the

box

children

Riverhead Books a member of Penguin Putnam Inc. New York 2002

the

box

children

sharon wyse

"Little Orphant Annie" (p. 90) from James Whitcomb Riley, *Complete Works*, Memorial edn. in 10 vols. (Indianapolis: Bobbs-Merrill, 1916): V, 1169–72. PS 2700 F16 Robarts Library. Originally published as "The Elf Child" in *Indianapolis Journal* (Nov. 15, 1885).

RIVERHEAD BOOKS
a member of
Penguin Putnam Inc.
375 Hudson Street
New York, NY 10014

Library of Congress Cataloging-in-Publication Data

Wyse, Sharon.
  The box children / by Sharon Wyse.
    p.   cm.
  ISBN 1-57322-219-4
    1. Girls—Fiction.   2. Farm life—Fiction.   3. Texas,West—Fiction.
    I. Title.
PS3623.Y74 B69   2002   2001057883
813'.6—dc21

Printed in the United States of America
10 9 8 7 6 5 4 3 2 1

This book is printed on acid-free paper. ♾

Book design by Chris Welch

to David
and to Glen

I can put my eyes just at the top of the wheat and see the world stretch out flat to the sky. All around me is the land we farm. I can see a cloud of dust that I know is Daddy on the red tractor in the field on one side of the house. My brother is on a green tractor on the other side. They plow the ground where no wheat is planted this year. After a rain the weeds start to grow and you have to plow them up fast before they take hold. There is one kind called bindweed that takes over everything no matter how many times you plow. The only way to get rid of it is to poison deep down. You have to just kill the whole field, then wait until it's safe again for something to live there. It can take years.

Back at the house Mother is sewing me another dress. She makes perfect dresses but she hates to sew. I feel it when she fits the pattern to my chest. Her sharp fingers dig the thin paper into my side and she sets her lips to hold the pins tight between them. She is fierce in her sewing. She makes the machine tear through my new dress, faster, faster. It will be done soon and time to try it on so she can mark the hem. Stand still! she will say. She sticks me if I move.

The wheat is yellow-green, almost ripe. If I took out walking east, away from the house, I'd get to Oklahoma pretty quick. It's only seven miles, but walking through the wheat would not be easy or fun. There's no path and the wheat is scratchy from my ankles all the way up to my chest.

Still, I think about it.

Mother says to be happy with what I've got. It's true that our family is better than most. We have a mother, a daddy, and two children: one boy, one girl. We are all smart but not too smart for our own good. The daddy goes to church every week with the family instead of staying home or only going on Christmas and Easter. The children mind and never talk back. The only place we ever get in trouble is at home.

What you are reading is my diary.

I have started it just to see what will happen. I will have to be careful. Mother hunts through my room all the time to make sure I'm not hiding things from her. Her rule is Never write anything down because you never know who will see it. That rule won't work for me. I want to write everything down and I want people to see it. Not her, but other people. People I don't know yet.

I have saved up some tracing paper and some pages from a drawing tablet my cousins in Oklahoma gave me when we visited them at Christmas. I have almost half of a spiral notebook left over from fifth grade, which I'm no longer in. Also, one of my jobs is taking out the trash and I can probably find things that will do for writing paper there too, before I burn it all up.

There's an upside-down barrel behind the bunkhouse, out by the junkpile where nobody ever goes. I found two big flat rocks that I have put under the barrel. I can put my diary papers on top of one rock and use the other rock to hold them down, then cover it all with the barrel.

Harvest is only a few weeks away. Until then my writing place is right here in the wheat. The ground is hard dirt and there are black beetles crawling all around. My plan is to come here and write every afternoon when I finish the noon dishes. Mother expects me quiet while she drinks a beer and takes her nap. Once I woke her up and she yanked me right off the floor by my ears. Now I stay outside until she rings the dinner bell to get me back.

My name is Lou Ann Campbell. I am almost twelve years old. Wish me luck!

Thursday, June 2, 1960

I will start with this: Mother is going to have a baby.

She has tried to have babies before, five other ones. Two before my brother, one between him and me, and two after me. I only know about them because one time I asked Mother how come she didn't have more kids. She said she had seven but only my brother and I made it out alive. She said the rest of her babies are ghosts and I'll be one too someday. I asked her if they had funerals for the ghost babies and she said Don't be silly, people don't do that. She said, Forget I told you.

But I couldn't forget. I started having dreams about them. They said they were happy, they said we could be friends. I made a box up like a bed and I put five plastic dolls in it. I decided that two were boys and three were girls. I made up their names: Mike and Jim, Jody, Molly, and Sally. We play. Mother knows I have them but I don't think she knows who they are.

Now a new one is on the way. There is no way to know if it will make it.

I have been the baby of this family for a long time. It would be just fine with me to give that up. I would feel like Miss America turning over her crown. I've had a lot of experience, and I would know how to help somebody get through it.

I think it should be a boy. I would be one if I could. Good boys do fine always. Every good boy does fine. I learned those at my piano lessons to remember the names of the lines in the bass clef and treble clef.

I made up these for girls:

Girls buy donuts for aunts.
Every girl buys donuts fresh.

My piano teacher says I should learn things the way they are taught to me.

Friday, June 3, 1960

My brother's name is Will. He just turned fourteen but he's been driving the John Deere since he was ten. This summer he started sleeping out in the bunkhouse with the hired hands. They have all carved their initials on the walls and there are pinups of ladies in underwear. I'm not supposed to go out there but sometimes I do. Will used to help me with the dishes but I told him he shouldn't, even before he started being one of the men. I said, You're a boy like Daddy and boys don't help with dishes. He said You're right and he told Mother and she told Daddy and he said You're right and my brother never had to help again.

On Saturdays when we don't have to work, Mother takes me and Will for ice cream cones at the drug store in Bussard. We spend all our allowance on funny books. He buys Superman, Batman, and Green Lantern. I get Casper and Archie. We read them on the way home, then we read them again on the back porch bed, then we trade. Then we put them on the pile with all the other funny books we have. It's a tall pile and we forget about the ones on the bottom. When we read them over again it's like they were new almost.

Will taught me to stick marshmallows on coat hangers and hold them over the fire when we burn the trash. He holds his marshmallow way up where the air is hot but there's no flame. It takes a long time, but his marshmallows always come out puffy and golden. I go right for the burning and mine is boiling black in seconds. I eat off the top layer of ash and stick the gooey white part back in the fire. I eat three sweet burnt layers off each marshmallow while my brother waits for perfection.

When we were little, we used to climb up in the wheat truck and pretend to go to Kansas City. Will would be the driver and I'd be the wife. He'd turn the big steering wheel back and forth and I'd watch out the window for road robbers. One time I asked him if we could get married when we grew up, but he told me brothers and sisters don't do that. I just meant that I like him more than any other boy. At the dinner table we can just look at each other and start laughing so hard we get in trouble.

Last week we went to the picture show by ourselves while Mother and Daddy went to a party at the Watsons' in town. In the movie, people kept coming to stay at a scary old house and then dying before the night was over. They climbed some rickety stairs in the dark and fell into a big acid pit at the top. The acid boiled up around them and ate up everything but their bones. I saw their skin and muscles fizz away. Every time the people started climbing the stairs, I screamed and screamed to warn them. I grabbed my brother's hand and we both squeezed hard.

When the movie was over and the lights came on, the room was still shadowy. I was sure there was something behind the curtains. I grabbed Will's hand again but he didn't squeeze back. He made his voice deep and said Stop it, the show's over. We walked over to the Watsons' house in the dark. I was afraid the street gravel would turn to quicksand like I have seen in other movies. I wanted to run but Will said it wouldn't help. He said he wasn't afraid.

He's had more practice in the dark. Every night he goes out into it to turn off the windmill. Daddy makes him say I'm not afraid I'm not afraid I'm not afraid I'm not afraid. I can hear my brother yell it louder and louder as he gets farther out into the night. I hear the windmill's metal moan when he pulls the wooden bar down. It takes his whole weight swinging on the bar to stop the turning and he fastens it down with wire and runs yelling I'm not afraid I'm not afraid all the way back to the door breathing hard and Daddy says There now that wasn't so bad was it, and my brother says No sir.

Saturday, June 4, 1960

About my Daddy. He has shiny black hair with a wave in front and greenish eyes so pale they look almost white when we're out in the sun. Mother wants us to call him

"Father" because it sounds more educated, but Daddy says no. He says it makes him sound like The Lord.

He works hard and only drinks at parties. Sometimes on the mornings after, he stays in bed late and tells my brother and me funny stories with our names in them. He rubs his rough whiskers on our necks and growls Gimme some sugar! He pretends his two fingers are Creep Mouse and Tickle Mouse and he walks them everywhere on us. We laugh so hard we cry, but there is no way to stop the Mouse Twins until Daddy is finished.

Sometimes he gets on his knees and rambles around pretending he's my horsey. He tries to buck me off but I hold on tight with my legs. After a while his voice gets gruff and he says Alright that's enough now. If I don't get off right then, he gets up fast and dumps me on the floor. Grabbing back on just makes him mad. The same thing happens when he says Come sit on my lap. He says Trotta Ma Horse and Go To Town! He bucks me hard and I laugh. Then he has had enough.

I want to be the kind of girl my Daddy will play with forever. I don't want him to ever get tired of me. I don't want him to ever get mad at me. There must be a way to make him play longer but I haven't found it yet. I just have to always be ready when he is or else there is no fun with my Daddy at all.

Even when he plays rough I'm sorry when it's over.

He likes to scare me. Last summer I was getting ready for bed and I heard scritch-scratching on the screen outside. I ran into Daddy and Mother's bedroom to tell but only Mother was in there. Then in came Daddy all out of breath. He said he heard a burglar out there and went to run him off. I know better.

Another time I was almost asleep when my mattress started moving up and down in the middle. I screamed and when Mother ran in, Daddy crawled out from under the bed laughing. I have thought about it since and I wonder how long he'd been hiding under there. Now before I change my clothes I check under the bed first.

Daddy is worried about my fat ankles. He thought they would get thinner when I got taller but that's not happening. I have heard him during Miss America saying, That one would be real pretty if it weren't for her ankles. I do exercises with my feet going in a circle but nothing changes. Lots of people say I have pretty eyes so I try to keep them looking there.

Daddy has a rule about food and the hired hands: When they are working, they eat every meal with us, breakfast, dinner and supper, meat and potatoes at every meal, all hot, no sandwiches. Sometimes Mother wants to try out a recipe like Chicken Cacciatore from a magazine but Daddy won't have it. He says food is one of the most important things for keeping husbands and good help. He wants us to cook such good food and so much of it that the men will cry from missing it if they ever leave. He says he sure would.

He comes in from the field at night with dirt thick all over him. He rubs himself hard with Lava soap and leaves the lavatory brown. When he's done I scrub the field dirt down the drain and change the towels. I even scrub the soap bar. It amazes me that soap itself can get dirty.

Every now and then Daddy decides to teach me a lesson. Not because I did something wrong but so I won't make mistakes in the future. In the bunkhouse he made me puff on his big cigar til I nearly coughed myself to death to teach me not to smoke. He made me watch him cut the dead babies out from the inside of a dead mama jackrabbit to teach me that it's stupid to care about wild animals. Out in the barn he showed me a nest of pink baby mice, then crunched them flat with his boot. Mice mess in the seed wheat, he said.

These lessons make me cry but I stop when he calls me Whiney Pot. He says Don't carry on unless you want trouble. I don't. I have never wanted trouble.

At church there is a girl I like, Alva Higgins, who comes all by herself. She always has on the same dress and her hair is straight and dirty. All the things Mother does to make me look good, no one does for her. She sits way in the back. She's only around in the summers when her daddy is a hired hand for Charlie Hillabolt. Her skin is dark tan like mine will never be. People say her mama is a Mexican. I asked Alva if her mama is a Mexican but she said she doesn't have a mama.

Alva is the only person I know who doesn't smile. She just does not do it. She looks at everything straight on and she answers questions right out without adding the smile. You might think that she would look mad or grumpy but it doesn't come out that way. It comes out like she knows everything and isn't worried about anything. Some pictures of Jesus look like that.

I asked Alva if she wanted to come out to our house next week after church. She said Did you ask your mama? I said No not yet. She said Well, she won't let me come over. No one's mama does. I said Why not? She said Just because. You can try but you'll see.

I told her I would try. She said, You know my daddy can't come and pick me up, he's sleeping and besides we don't have a car. It didn't make Alva ashamed to say that. It would me.

When we got home from church the whole house smelled like the roast Mother had put in the oven before we left. I peeled the potatoes and Mother put them in to boil. While she was cutting up tomatoes I asked her: Can Alva come over after church next week? She said Who's Alva? I said Alva Higgins, from church. She said No Higginses go to our church. I said Alva does, she comes by herself. Mother said, You don't mean that dirty little Mexican girl? I said, I don't think she's Mexican. She's just tan.

Listen to me, Mother said. She pointed her knife at me the way teachers do chalk. She said Alva Higgins is trash. Her daddy is a drunk and her mama is a hore. You don't know what that is yet but men sure do. Alva will be one herself soon enough, you watch. I am the only one who will tell you the truth about these things. And I am not fixing any Sunday dinner for any Higgins.

Well then can I go over to her house, I asked.

With the knife in her hand, Mother knocked hard into my head with her elbow. I wasn't expecting it so I fell right over.

Standing over me she said, You think you know everything. Well learn this: If a white horse goes through a mud puddle, the mud puddle does not turn white. There is nothing you can get from Alva Higgins that a decent white person would want. Did you wash your hands before you peeled those potatoes?

Yes ma'am, I said. When she is mad, sometimes yes ma'am will get her over it. Or else she will say Don't yes ma'am me, and it makes it worse. This time it made her forget what we were even talking about. She just turned around and went back to the tomatoes and told me nice to set the table please now.

She is wrong, though. I don't think I know everything. There's way too much I don't know. But I do know that Alva was right, my mama isn't going to let her come. There is no point in trying again.

Monday, June 6, 1960

We don't own the land we farm. Mother's daddy does, him and his two sisters. We call him Daddy Wayne. He is married to Nanny Wayne. They will be up for harvest, and probably my great aunts too.

I wish we farmed land closer to a big town. The closest town to us is Bussard. It's right on the railroad, near Kiowa Creek. Outside the town is a sign that says "God

Welcomes You to Bussard, Texas" and then under that, "Population 204." Most of the population doesn't live in actual Bussard though. Most are farmers like us. We live nine miles out. We come to town for groceries, the bank, the drug store, the picture show, the Legion Hall, and church. It's all on one street.

The main feature of Bussard is the grain elevator. I can see it from here, white and waving a little bit from the heat. Sometimes I can see the elevators of other towns too, farther away. Every town next to the railroad has one. At harvest we bring our wheat to the Bussard elevator. Then trains come and take it away for the rest of the country to make bread with. We feed a lot of people.

Farther away is a big town called Wheatly, population 4,409. We go there for the shopping center and the doctor. I used to think it was named for the wheat all around, but it's not. It's for a rich family there. Wheatly just happened to be their name, which no one can help.

At the grocery store in Wheatly there's a boy who puts the groceries in bags and carries them to our car. He likes me. When he sees us checking out, he trades places with the boy who is bagging at our counter. He smiles right at me. I have to pretend not to notice and only smile when Mother is looking down to write out her check. She feels it anyway though and tells me to go on out and open the trunk and wait in the car. That way she walks out with the boy. Still, after the groceries are loaded and she is backing the car out, I wave to him with my little finger and he waves back.

Last time on the way home Mother said, Nice girls are very careful who they smile at. The time before that she said, If you let a boy look at you, you don't know what will happen next. Once she also said Boys from good families don't work in grocery stores.

When she says things like that, I don't say anything back. I like the way the air is stiff between us.

Tuesday, June 7, 1960

Mother says I have a tendency to be sick, she can tell by my bad breath. My stomach hurts almost every day and I get fevers a lot.

Every time I go to the bathroom and have a bm I have to call Mother so she can come look before I flush. Everything has to be just right because this is the key to health. The best color is brown, not too light, not too dark. It should be about like soft clay, not too hard, not too soft. There should not be too much of it. There should be one every day.

If I miss a day, she gives me a Caroid pill. If the bm is too hard or there is not enough of it, it's Ex-Lax. If it gets too loose then it's Pepto-Bismol, but that turns everything all dark so she has to get Daddy to help her give me an enema to clean it all out and start fresh. Other choices are Milk of Magnesia and Epsom Salts.

The worst thing is Castor Oil which I get if I have fever more than a day. I can vomit just from the smell. She gives it to me with root beer and says to hold my nose and keep my upper lip out of the oil when I drink. She says Swallow fast! If I throw it up, I have to take more until it stays down.

For two days I didn't call her to look at my bms. I thought she might forget but she remembered this morning. After she spanked me, she said I looked pale and that she would have to take me to the doctor to find out what is going on in there.

So after breakfast she put a pot of beef stew on low and took me over to Wheatly. She made me put my bm in a refrigerator dish because she said The doctor will want a stool sample. I carried it warm in my lap in a paper bag for the whole car ride.

In his office Dr. Healey took my temperature, listened to my heart, and had me breathe deep. He asked me if I had started men-something yet. I looked at Mother and she was shaking her head NO! so I said No I don't think so. He said, I think you would know for sure! He laughed but Mother didn't. Then he threw the stool sample in the trash without even opening it. He said, There is nothing wrong with this girl, Loretta. You're going to make a hipokondreeak out of her if you keep this up. And if I were you, I'd tell her about the curse, it won't be long now.

Dr. Healey is Mother's doctor for the baby too. So he said While you're here, why don't I check you out? She got up on the table and he listened where the baby is.

He listened all around and his face got worried. He said Lie down, Loretta, we might have a little problem here. He tried to help her lie back but she knocked him out of the way and was off the table fast. She said Come on Lou Ann, we got dinner to cook.

But instead of going straight home we went to the state line and got a six pack of beer. Mother started drinking it before we were out of the parking lot. She looked at me hard and said, Nothing that man said is true. Don't ask me any questions and don't tell your father a thing. There is nothing to tell. Do you hear me?

I said I did. But I didn't understand. What is the curse? Something about men. What is it? Do I have it? Will I die soon?

The doctor said, There is nothing wrong with this

girl. I keep hearing that in my head over and over. Nothing wrong, nothing wrong.

But Mother said nothing he said is true. She says she is the only one who always tells me the truth. She says other people will lie just to make me feel better.

I would like to feel better.

Wednesday, June 8, 1960

Out by the road on the far side of the house is a wild rose bush. It's mostly thorns. We never water it or cut it back. It just lives on its own. It makes tiny pale yellow roses that never relax. I think the buds know that opening up is the beginning of the end. The open rose edges turn brown quick, then the petals curl in and fall off. All summer long there are roses in every stage—closed tight, open but worried, brown, curled, and gone. We never cut them for show because it isn't worth it. The flowers are too small and not pretty enough.

I don't know where the bush came from. We don't plant flowers. All our energy goes into growing food. Wheat is the main thing, but we also grow cherries, peaches, cucumbers, tomatoes, onions, lettuce, beans, and squash. It's so dry and dusty here that everything in the garden has to be watered every day. I run a hose from the windmill across the driveway and into the garden, 15 minutes on each row.

It was fun when my brother used to do the watering with me. While we'd wait for each row to get wet, he'd make smooth dirt roads with the hoe and bring his cars and trucks out to race. He'd make vroom sounds when the winner crossed the finish line.

Now I just set the timer and go in the house to wait where it's cooler.

I'd like to water the rose bush but Daddy says it's a waste of water. How can that be true? Every spring when the new buds come, I am amazed. Through ice and snow and freezing wind the bush is always back with thorns and green growing.

Thursday, June 9, 1960

Mother keeps me busy all the time. The devil can't get me if I'm doing something worthwhile, she says. After breakfast she gives me a hanger and a bag with plastic to braid onto it so our clothes won't get rusty. She wants the hangers perfect. No knots, no messups. I have done a whole hanger over because of an early messup I didn't see sooner.

When I see the hangers in my closet I hate them. I hate that my own hands did them without wanting to.

Sometimes I think about the idea of wanting to, what that is made out of. For example I used to like to stand on the bed and bounce a few times and then jump off. But once when I did that Mother was hitting me by the time I landed. I don't even know where she came from. So now when I think of jumping on the bed I don't want to do it any more even though I know it would be fun.

Sometimes you have to want something a long time before you can figure out a way to do it, like with this diary.

Last night I had a dream about the new baby. I opened my closet door and he was in there in the shoebox next to the others. He was sick but still alive. He was made of clear plastic and I could see through to all his blood vessels, red and blue. He was having trouble breathing. There was a tiny tube coming out of his chest and I blew into it. It worked! He wiggled around like a real baby and smiled. But then I had to keep doing it or he would die.

I told the box children about my dream. They are worried and so am I. They do not want more company. It's too crowded in that box already.

Friday, June 10, 1960

Mother wants a new refrigerator but Daddy says no. She has wanted one for as long as I can remember. She cuts out pictures from Life magazine and makes lists of the features she is looking for. Daddy says as long as the milk is cold that's enough. We have a deep freeze on the back porch that can hold a whole cut-up cow. But she wants more convenience.

Our refrigerator is just a cold white box with metal shelves. Every other day my job is to take everything out and wipe it all clean with Jubilee including the jars and refrigerator dishes. If ice has built up, I chip it off. If anything has gone bad I throw it away. Daddy gets mad if he sees old bad food in there.

Mother says with the new baby coming she will need me for other things besides keeping frost and germs off of her refrigerator. She says the new refrigerators have freezers that defrost themselves, fans that purify the air inside, and ultra-violent rays that kill the germs. They have doors with shelves and magnetic latches to keep children from getting shut inside. They make ice cubes for you, keep your vegetables crunchy, and soften up your butter.

In Life magazine, the mothers stand next to their refrigerators in tight fancy dresses and pearl necklaces. They have on party smiles and their fingernails are long and painted. Their kitchens are from the future. New everything.

In our kitchen Mother cooks and cleans wearing the dresses she makes for everyday, sleeveless and straight, out of leftover material. They just go right over her head like sacks. Sometimes the arm holes are cut too big and I can see more than I want to.

But when there is a dance at the Legion Hall, Mother looks like the ladies in the magazine. She wears a blue shiny dress so tight she has to wear a girdle bra down to her waist. She has me fasten the hooks while she plumps her bosoms up high. She wears a necklace made of crystals, and high heels you can see through. She puts dark red on her lips and asks me if there is any on her teeth after she blots. She has me roll her hair up in pincurls, comb it out, and spray it stiff. When she is finished she's beautiful.

The day after the dance it's always hard seeing her at the stove in her sack dress. Sometimes her lips are still a little red. Sometimes she hums a song and does a little dance step. Other times she stirs the pot so hard I know something is wrong. When I ask she says Your Daddy forgot who he came to the dance with.

It's strange to be writing out here in the field at a different time from usual. I woke up early and Mother and Daddy were still sleeping. On the table by the back door I saw a nice pad of smooth paper with lines and I tore off quite a bit for my diary. I don't think Daddy will ever miss it.

It's so quiet. The morning sky is gray with pink and the air has a chill on it.

I have brought the box children out with me. They need some fresh air and I need some company. They like to walk all around in between the wheat stalks. I'm having them be in a play. Here is what they say:

Mike: What a beautiful day! The sun is brighter than a hundred shiny lemons.

Jim: Brighter than all the stars together.

Jody: Bright as gold.

Molly: Bright as diamonds.

Sally: Bright as a new baby's eyes.

Mike: Speaking of babies, what do you think is going on with the Mother and the new one?

Jim: I don't know. Is she showing yet?

Me: Not really. But it's still early.

Jody: Maybe it's just a tiny tiny baby.

Molly: Maybe the baby is all folded up.

Sally: Maybe the baby is waiting to see if it wants to grow or not.

Mike: I think the baby needs our help.

Jim: Then we've got to help it! The Mother needs this baby.

Mike: What can we do?

Jody: Don't let her lift heavy things.

Molly: Don't let her reach way up into cabinets.

Sally: Make her rest more in bed.

Mike: But she tried all that with us and we still died. We have to do something better. How about magic?

Jim: Do you know how to do it?

Jody: Abracadabra.

Molly: Pudding and pie.

Sally: Open sesame!

Me: I think those are just pretend magic. But I could ask Alva Higgins if she knows magic. Or I could get a book from the library in Wheatly. Or I could make something up and if we all believe, maybe it will work.

ALL DOLLS: Hurray! We will save the baby!

In real life, I don't feel as happy as the dolls do. I only said that about the magic to make them feel better.

There are things I haven't told them about the way Mother is with babies. A lot of mothers come to ask her for advice because my brother and I are turning out so well.

The main thing she says is: "You have to break the baby's will from the very first minute. After that you'll never have a day of trouble." Mothers bring their babies out here for several days in a row for Mother to toilet train. She gets them out of diapers before they are one year old.

I watched her with Velmarie Tucker's girl whose name is Veleen. Mother gave Veleen lots of milk and then took her diaper off and sat and watched. When anything started to come out, Mother hit Veleen there and said Bad bad baby. She kept hitting while she ran Veleen over to the little potty her mother had brought. Then she held Veleen hard onto the potty. By then Veleen was crying pretty wild and forgot whatever all it was she needed to do.

Mother said Come on now, quit that crying, this is what big girls do, be a good girl, only bad babies mess their diapers. Finally after Veleen couldn't hold it in any longer the water or bm came out. She was still crying. Mother said Good good baby and gave her a spoon of sugar water, then danced her all around the room. That made Veleen laugh and laugh. Then the whole thing started over.

After the third day Veleen would get a terrible look on her face whenever she needed to do something down there. Mother would say, Good Veleen need to go potty? and Veleen would crawl right over there herself. If she didn't quite get there soon enough though, she would get hit.

Mothers ask Mother how she does it, but they don't really want the answer and she doesn't give it to them. I know that what she did with Veleen she did with me too, and with my brother. I still clutch those muscles there all the time. I can't help it.

I understand about the box children wanting to help the baby while it's still inside Mother. That's all they remember. But I don't figure there's much I can do about that. I am already thinking about what to do when it comes out, how to help it then.

I let the children play in the dirt for a while longer. If they were real, think how much fun we would have.

Sunday, June 12, 1960

The termite man was here when we got home from church. He comes once every summer to spray the foundation of our house and look for damage all over. We are some of his best customers because we call him even if we don't have money to spare. Daddy says with a wooden house you don't have a choice. The outside of the wood can look just fine while the inside is being nibbled rotten. Our preacher uses termite stories to show how the devil works on souls.

There are other things that can take a house down. Tornadoes, for instance. Sometimes when we're out driving we come to places where all that's left of what used to be a house is the front porch steps. They head up to nowhere, one two three.

Another thing that can get a house is time, if you just let it. Down the road is a house that has been empty for twenty-five years, since the woman who lived there went crazy. The house still belongs to her and she won't sign the papers for tearing it down. It bothers Daddy to see such a ramshackle place. He gets rid of things fast once he decides they can't be fixed, like plowing a crop under the day after a hailstorm or killing a cat with a bad eye infection.

l understand the old woman, though. What else does she have? Sometimes I walk down there and look all around. Weeds are growing inside the house where the floor is crumbled. There are plates and cups and saucers in the falling-down cabinets, and bits of curtain hanging where the windows were. Outside, all the paint is off and the wood has gone gray and soft.

I am watching close to see how long it takes for things to fall apart on their own.

Monday, June 13, 1960

We have a swimming tank ten feet high and twenty feet across, made out of thick curved metal pieces bolted together. It's the same thing ranchers use to make water tanks for their cattle but no one else has made a whole big swimming pool out of it. In this way we are famous. Every Fourth of July, farm families from all around come to our house to celebrate the end of harvest and to swim.

It takes about three weeks for the tank to fill up after the weather turns warm. We leave the windmill pumping day and night. It makes a light air and metal circle sound while the wind blows steady and hot. The drinking water tank fills up first and then overflows into the swimming tank.

I run out every morning before breakfast to check how high it is and to watch the water splash in. As soon as the bottom is covered with water I climb down the sharp little metal ladder inside and jump in. The tank walls are so high my voice makes echoes. When the tank is full all the way to the top I can see out over everything. I can close my eyes and pretend the sound of the wheat is a big ocean.

The hired hands take their baths wearing swimsuits in the tank. From the back porch I watch them climb out shivery and run barefoot to the bunkhouse in the night wind. Les Riffle has red curly hair on his chest and legs. Buck Davis has black hair growing all over his back, too. Les and Buck have been with us every summer since I was born. Lonnie Helfenbein is new. He is only sixteen and his chest is white and smooth like my brother's, like mine.

Daddy taught me to swim in the tank when I was five and the water was up to his waist. He picked me up with his hand under my belly and said Swim! Every now and then he would let go of me and I would sink and sputter. He kept saying This time you'll get it. Every day the water got higher and Daddy got more ready for me to do it right. Swim! Swim! I did all the things that look like swimming but I still went under. Swim! Water came into my mouth and nose. Things got dizzy. When Daddy pulled me up all I could do was cough and cry. I wanted to quit but he said Quitters never learn. He said Try again.

I finally learned to stay up but I'm not very good. Swimming tires me out. I keep my head above the water and try not to open my mouth or breathe much so no water will get in. Mostly I sit inside a big innertube from a tractor tire. I love to float.

Tuesday, June 14, 1960

I have a pen pal named Wyn Rue. I got her from the church office where they have a list of other Methodist girls who want to write letters. She is from Oklahoma City and she is my age.

Before Wyn, I never had fun with letters. I would start out with How are you? I am fine. After that there didn't seem to be much else to say. Besides, Mother reads all my letters, the ones that come in and the ones that go out. She won't give me a stamp until she is happy with the letter. If she doesn't like what I said or if I misspell a word she makes me re-write the whole thing because she says crossouts are messy and messy letters are rude.

Wyn writes "Ha!" a lot in her letters and she writes "alot" as all one word. She has lots of crossouts which Mother says is an example of how she isn't being brought up right. Also Wyn lives in a big city and people don't know how to act right there. For these reasons Mother makes her lips tight whenever I get a letter from Wyn or when she gives me the stamp for my answer. She can't do much else because after all this was the church's idea. Still, if I didn't like Wyn so much, those lips would be enough to make me not write. Tight lips have stopped me on a lot of things.

Wyn draws funny pictures of her family and tells me when she has a crush on a cute boy. She tells me what foods she likes to eat and about her favorite songs on the radio. She has her own record player in her room and she has 2 brown cocker spaniels that sleep right in bed with her.

I tell her things about the farm mostly. What my jobs are, about the wheat getting ripe, about the swimming tank, about my brother driving a tractor. I told her I take piano lessons from the preacher's wife during school. She thinks these things are interesting. She says maybe we can visit each other someday. I want to write her about the new baby on the way but I can't until Mother is ready to tell. I thought maybe since Wyn lives in a whole other state it would be OK, but Mother says everybody tells your secret to just one other friend and pretty soon the entire world knows.

Without Wyn and this diary, life would just be going by with no record, like no one knew a thing.

Wednesday, June 15, 1960

Mother takes baths with me to save water. She runs it hot and says Come get in. Yesterday she woke up from her nap early and ran the bath because we had to go to a mother-and-daughter dressup birthday party for a girl in my Sunday School class.

In the tub my job is to soap up the washcloth till it is white and foamy. Mother takes it all over her own body first, scrub scrub scrub. She always says the same things: Wash under your breasts or you will have that sourness. Wash under your arms or you will get B.O. Wash your fronty because it stinks down there. When she says that, she pushes her bottom up out of the water and scrubs between her legs where the curly hair is. Then she tells me Stand up. She scrubs my back and arms and legs and says Turn around. She does my tummy and says Put your legs apart. She scrubs my fronty hard for a long time. She says Dirty, dirty, dirty. I think of other things until finally she stops. All clean! she says. Sit down and rinse off.

Yesterday after we dried off, she went to her room and I went to mine. My newest dress was all laid out, palest green with the flowers she embroidered. I was supposed to put on my underwear and petticoat and dress and then sit still until she came to button me up and tie the bow perfect in back. But I couldn't. I was too hot all over from the scrubbing. I crawled under the bed with my whole body on the cool wood. Cool on my face, my stomach, my legs. I was holding my fronty tight because it wanted that.

Mother's high heels sounded far away. She will never find me in this cool dark place, is what I thought.

I was wrong. She grabbed me out from under the bed and started hitting me with both her hands. She hit me down the hallway and kept going until she wore herself out. She said Bad girl bad girl bad bad girl. Then she pushed me into my clothes and said Because of you we are going to be late. She gave me a cold washrag and said Hold this on your face, it will take the red out.

In the car my bones hurt like they were going to explode. When that happens I hold everything still and just wait. It feels impossible but I do it. At the party only Weena Willis asked me if I had been crying. I've seen her look that way herself so I just said Yes. She didn't ask why. She said my dress was so pretty.

It is a very pretty dress.

Thursday, June 16, 1960

Yesterday evening Mother called me into her bedroom. She was lying there on top of the quilt with no lights on. She said Come lie down here and have a talk. Take your shoes off first.

She said: You are going to start bleeding every month. It is called ministration. It will take the blood out of your lips so you will have to start wearing lipstick. You will have cramps and you will want to scream but don't you dare. Some girls squirm all around and moan but it's better to lie still and keep quiet. You can't go swimming. And don't call it the curse. Only sinners question God's ways. When your time comes I don't want a word of trouble. You are a very lucky girl. When I was little we had to wear smelly old rags but now there are modern sanitary conveniences.

I said, Where does the blood come out of?

Down there, she said.

Fronty or hiney? I asked.

She didn't answer me. She said: Once you start to bleed, bad things can happen. Boys will try to get you. They will say it feels good but it only hurts. A girl who isn't married keeps her legs together. A girl who ruins her reputation is better off dead. Do you understand?

I said Yes ma'am but do you still bleed even though you're married? She said We are not talking about me.

I said Is this something about having babies?

She said You won't be having to worry about that unless you let some man stick his hard old thing in you. If that happens you better not ever show your face here again. This conversation is over now, she said.

I figure this is what Dr. Healey was talking about. At least I won't die.

But as far as I can tell, nothing good will ever happen between my legs. There will be three kinds of dirty stuff coming out and a place for boys and old men to hurt me.

In my dreams I am made just like my dolls, all shiny plastic down there with no holes at all.

Friday, June 17, 1960

I wrote Wyn Rue that our wheat is getting ripe. Everyday there is less green and more gold. Yesterday Daddy called our cutters and said, When can you come? They said one week. They cut their way north, right up through Texas, Oklahoma, Kansas and Nebraska with six combines, three trucks, and three trailer houses. Sometimes our wheat is ready before they get here and we worry every second. A year's worth of perfect ripe wheat can be lost to rain or hail or too much sun. Once they start, the cutters cut all day and all night to get the wheat in safe.

I like it when the cutters get here because life gets different. There are 14 more people to look at and think about. Our cutters are the Cumberlands, Amos and Viola. He's the boss and she cooks for the crew which we call Wheaties. They are like our hired hands except they like to travel. I would like that too, every few weeks a new place to call home. They sleep in trailer houses which they park out by the barn. In town, a bad way to tease a girl is to say, "Jenny went out with a Wheatie." If a girl really did that, it would ruin her reputation.

After harvest Daddy saves the best wheat for seed so he will have something to plant next year. He stores it in four big wooden bins built right into the barn. I love to climb in them. Even when it's hot outside, the wheat feels cool in the dark. It moves when you move. It makes you push hard and go slow like in a dream. I put my legs all the way in and it holds me up. Sometimes I just lie down on top of it and fall asleep. It's another world.

Saturday, June 18, 1960

I keep learning new things every day.

After breakfast Mother took Will and me over to Wheatly to get Daddy presents for Father's Day which is tomorrow. We got him two packs of hankerchiffs and a pair of cacky pants. It's always the same. Mother says it's best to use special days to get things people need anyway. It keeps them from being prideful and thinking they are too important.

After we got the presents we went to the food store where the grocery bag boy works. He got in our line like always and while Mother signed the check I did a new smile I've been practicing, where I hold my head down and make my eyes look up.

Mother sent Will on ahead to open the trunk while we waited for the bag boy to pack the sacks. When we walked out, the bag boy got up close behind me and said Hey, what's your name? Before I could answer, Mother jumped in and said Coffee! Penny Coffee. The boy said, That's a pretty name, Penny. Real polite. Mother smiled sweet and said, Why don't you go on back inside the store, young man? My son is perfectly able to load up these groceries, thank you very much.

While Will put the bags in the trunk, Mother explained that Penny Coffee was a person she knew when she was young, and that she always used that name for protection when she didn't want to give somebody her real name. She said Never give strangers your real name or they might find out where you live.

Will smiled mean and said, Hey Penny! Who's your new boyfriend? Mother said, There's nothing new about any of this.

But actually there is something new: Mother told a lie and acted like it's a good thing to do if you have a good reason. Until now it always meant you were evil.

Another new thing is that the boy believed it. She always said If you tell a lie it shows on your face and everyone knows.

So now I am thinking about lying. I know that my brother kissed Karen Slaney at a hayride last summer, but when Mother asked him if he had fun he said no. He said he didn't talk to anybody all night. She said, Don't worry, before long you will have more girls than you know what to do with. If he had told the truth she would have said, You better look out, Buster, or you'll have more trouble than you can handle.

Both of the things she said end up with Will in trouble but the lie one is much nicer.

Sunday, June 19, 1960

Daddy likes his Father's Day presents. Unless he was lying. "Ha!"

In a dream I had last night I climbed up into a tree and the branches kept on growing and growing so that when I climbed down I was miles away from home. I woke up happy. I wish I could feel like that all the time. But Daddy has a saying: Wish in one hand and shit in the other and see which one gets full faster.

Rev. Eubank says to pray to God for help instead of wishing. At night Mother makes me pray with her: Now I lay me down to sleep, I pray the lord my soul to keep, If I should die before I wake, I pray the lord my soul to take. I never say that prayer on my own. I just think of the moon and the stars and the box children. I bless them and they bless me. No one takes anyone's soul.

I have seen prayer not work more times than I have seen it work. Last summer we had a new white kitten and I was out watering the garden and I didn't know she was under a squash leaf and I was doing a little jumping dance and she ran out under my foot and I came down on her head. She screeched and started jerking all over. Her head stuck out on one side. I started praying right there, Oh God I'm sorry please don't let my kitty die, don't let her die, don't let her die. But she did die, and fast, with her eyes open looking right at me. I cried so hard that Daddy said I can't have another kitty till I'm old enough to know not to get too attached to them.

I will never be that old.

I have never actually gotten anything I prayed for. On the other hand, I have gotten a lot of things that I would never have even thought to ask for. Like the sky. There it just is. And dirt. What a great amazing thing to add water to. Even tornadoes. Who would imagine clouds and wind making a whirling air tunnel? It's a real wonder. Of course it's true that so far it has not been my house that got blown away.

I wish no one had ever told me about God. I would

just worship the world straight out. It wouldn't need to know me or love me or watch me. Just let me be here in it until my time is up.

I have a best friend named Betsy Roker. She lives on a farm on the far side of Bussard and in the summer I don't see that much of her. She has red hair, not the orangy kind but the kind that's almost maroon. Her parents and two older sisters have it too. She's a year younger than I am, but we're usually in the same class because the Bussard school has three grades together in the same room with the same teacher.

The main thing we do when we go to each other's houses is play "Tom and Sue." I'm Tom and she's Sue. They're in love. We act out the stories from Betsy's sister's romance books, but without the kissing.

What usually happens is that Sue is always getting into trouble because other guys make her think they're better than Tom. They say they have more money or will take Sue fancier places. They say things like, "Come on honey, we'll paint the town red." Because I'm a year older, I had to tell Betsy that they just meant to have a wild time and not really to use red paint. I also had to tell her how to pronounce pizza, although I have never eaten any. Alva Higgins taught me how to say it. She says it's just tomato pie.

I like being Tom. He's strong and he always wins Sue back because he is the smartest and nicest.

Betsy goes to church over in Wheatly because she's Catholic and we don't have that church in Bussard. Mother says the only difference between Catholics and Methodists is that Catholics have more babies. I asked Betsy about that and she said there are a lot of other differences. So we had a contest to see which one came out ahead.

She started out: OK, do you believe in God? Catholics believe in God. I said, So do Methodists. One point each.

Then it was my turn. I asked if she believed in Jesus. She said yes. Two points each.

Then she asked if I believed in the Virgin Mary and I said not so much, I mean yes but we don't make a big deal about it. So three for her, two and a half for me.

I asked her if they believed in Heaven and Hell and she said yes. Since it was a double question, that made it five for her, four and a half for me. She asked me if we made confession and I said I didn't know what that was.

She told me, and pulled ahead with six points to my four and a half. I asked her if they had communion and she said yes (seven to five and a half).

I couldn't think of any more questions so she asked if we gave up things for Lent, if we had nuns, and if our preachers wore robes. All of that put her way over the top with ten points.

Based on these results I have to agree with Betsy that the Catholics offer more as a religion, if that's what you are looking for. And if Mother is right about them having more babies, I don't see why she wouldn't want to just switch on over. Seems like she would want every advantage.

Tuesday, June 21, 1960

I had a bad scare yesterday.

Mother rang the bell when I was almost out to the barrel where I hide my diary, and she saw me. I thought fast and stuck the writing in my underwear like I was tucking my shirt tail in. When I walked in past her she grabbed my cheek in a pinch and looked in my eyes and said What's way out there that is any of your business?

At first I said Nothing, but when she yanked the pinch

harder I said A dead jackrabbit with its head eaten off. She said Did you touch it? I said Only the fur. She marched me by the cheek to the sink and handed me the soap. While I scrubbed she said How is it possible I got you for a daughter?

That is a good question.

Wednesday, June 22, 1960

Bad news. The cutters are coming in two days and last night it poured down rain for hours.

A cloud bank built up dark at the bottom of the sky just as the sun was going down. At supper Daddy said, I knew this crop was too good to last. The rain started at midnight and didn't let up till the sun came out this morning.

When the cutters get here there will be nothing for them to do but wait for the wheat to dry out. If the days stay hot and windy and there is no more rain, everything might still be OK, if we are lucky. But that's a big if.

Other things have happened too. Today Mother and Daddy drove the pickup into town to take care of some business. They let Will and me ride in the back. The pickup slid all over the muddy road and we fell around from one side to the other laughing like it was a county fair ride.

Daddy parked in town by the Equity Co-op. While we waited for him and Mother, Will sang me a song that the hired hands made up. He said not to tell. He was laughing so much I could hardly understand the words:

Underwear, underwear
Who can do without underwear?
I can do without underwear
But my dick says it's bad for my hair.

Hairy balls, hairy balls,
Who can do without hairy balls?
I can do without hairy balls
But then I couldn't be fuckin all the dolls.

On the way back I said Let's sing that song. He laughed and said You can't sing that song. I said Why not and he said Because you're a girl. I said Come on! and started singing it. Underwear, underwear, who can do without underwear, I can do without underwear, but then I couldn't remember the words of the last line. I asked him but he wouldn't tell me.

Come on! I said.

He said I'll sing it again by myself but not if you sing too. It's only a boy song. I said OK. He sang it. When he finished I started singing it but he yelled STOP IT!

Nobody said anything the rest of the way home.

In the bathtub last night I asked Mother What's fuckin? She said Where did you hear that word? I said From a song. She asked me to sing it for her. I said I couldn't because it's only a boy song. Who told you that? she said.

If my brother had not been mean to me I wouldn't have told.

She asked me again to sing it. She used her softest voice and said You can sing any song you want, sweetie. So finally I did. She got so interested in the song that she forgot to scrub me. She said it's good that I sang it for her.

But she didn't tell me what fuckin means. The truth is I think I kind of know. At breakfast and dinner today I didn't even look at Will and I don't think he looked at me either. I can't think of a time that's ever been true.

The new hired hand, Lonnie, doesn't talk unless Daddy asks him a question. He looks down when he answers and says Sir at the end. Les and Buck tease him for that but Daddy likes it.

Lonnie plays guitar. Sometimes if the fields are too wet to plow like they are now, he plays and sings all afternoon while Les and Buck are across the state line drinking and my brother goes all around with Daddy. Yesterday after I wrote in my diary I went over outside the bunkhouse door and heard Les doing an Everly Brothers song I like. I know the harmony to it and I started humming it quiet to myself.

He heard me. Who's out there? he said.

It's me, Lou Ann. I didn't mean to bother you. He came out and saw where I was. What are you doing out here? he said.

Just listening to you, I said. Don't tell Mother please. He said She don't want you coming out here? I said She'd spank me if she knew.

He said, Well I won't tell and I don't mind if you want to listen. Even singing along is OK with me if you like doing it. You want to come sit in here?

That is the most words I have ever heard Lonnie

Helfenbein say. I went into the bunkhouse and sat on a wooden crate. He sat on the side of his bed and did some more songs. The ones I knew, I sang along with. He said, That's real nice.

I left after a little while to be sure I would be out of there before Mother rang the bell. He said, You can come back any time you hear me playing.

I will do that. I wonder if he'd like to learn piano? I could teach him what I know.

Friday, June 24, 1960

The cutters showed up this morning early. They said they drove in mud the last 50 miles and that nobody's wheat is any drier than ours. That's good news. It means there's no reason for them not to stay right here and cut our wheat first.

But Daddy hates the waiting, and he hates us paying attention to the Wheaties. After breakfast he said he had to talk to me and Will, and I figured it would be about that.

Instead he said in his gruff voice that Mother had told him about the song Will taught me. He said Will would have to make his own paddle out of thick wood and would have to say how many licks he thinks he deserves. He said if Will ever says one word to me like I shouldn't have told on him, he will find out what's worse than spankings.

Will spent the rest of the day carving a paddle a whole inch thick. He didn't even come to dinner. A little before supper I saw him and Daddy heading out to the barn with the paddle, so I ran and hid outside to listen. Daddy said You are getting whipped here for being stupid. There's nothing wrong with singing a dirty song but you don't EVER do it in front of a lady.

Then he did the licks, ten of them. I saw my brother come out with a red face, slapping tears away before they had a chance to fall. At supper he kept his eyes on his plate the whole time. Mother made a point of saying The Lord has no use for people who pout. I felt a hard kick on my shin bone right then and it came from where Will was sitting. I didn't say one word.

The song he taught me is in my mind all the time. I picture the two of us in the back of the pickup laughing and sliding around. Now he hates me.

Mother says she's glad I'm her good girl. She says high morals will get a girl a lot farther than love.

Saturday, June 25, 1960

In a year when it didn't rain at the wrong time, harvest would already be over by now. We're very late. It wouldn't matter except that we like to finish by the 4th of July so we can have our bar-be-que to celebrate. We might not make it this year even if everything goes perfect from here on.

All there is to do is wait and hope for more days like today, hot and dry and windy. If you blew a fan through an oven it would feel like this.

Last night I looked out through the back porch window to where the cutters have parked their trailers and trucks and combines. I could see the Wheaties when they came out to smoke and talk and walk around. I could hear their deep voices.

Then early this morning Aunt Coleda showed up. She's Daddy Wayne's little sister. She drives up every summer at harvest to check on things since she owns some of the land. Her skin is oily and yellow and puffy, and she doesn't have much hair. She always has a cigarette in her mouth and she hides liquor in her suitcase. She wears perfume even though Mother is allergic. While she's here she stays in my bedroom and stinks it up, and I have to sleep out on the back porch bed. I have already moved the box children to a closet shelf out there so the cigarette smoke won't bother them.

She'll come in with a new dress on and ask, What do you think of this dress, Bill? Daddy never knows what to say because the dresses are always ugly and way too small. Coleda will say, "Size eight, on sale! That's my real size, you know." She wears gold bracelets that jangle when she taps her ashes. Her feet swell out over the top of her shoes and she slurs her steps the same way she does her words.

As soon as she gets here, she tells us to get in the car so she can have a look at her wheat. When she drives she pumps the gas pedal up and down. She never holds it any one place for more than a few seconds at a time. We jerk down the dirt roads to the part that is hers, then Daddy says Why don't I drive back so you can get a better look. Thank goodness she usually says OK.

Aunt Coleda only has a few things she says. It's different for each of us. When she likes something about Mother she says, "You're just like me, Loretta." To Daddy she says, "What do you think of this, Bill?" but she doesn't pay any attention to his answers. To my brother she says, "Give your Aunt Coleda a kiss, Willie." She kisses him right on the mouth. To me she says, "You should have seen me when I was your age. I was a beauty."

I do wish I could have seen her. I would like to know how that face could ever have been pretty, and if it was, how it got the way it is now. When I ask Mother if Aunt Coleda was a beauty she just makes a little face with one eyebrow raised.

But still Mother is nice to her. She lets her smoke in the house and she agrees with everything Aunt Coleda says even when I know she thinks different. I guess when people own your land you have to make sure they don't get mad at you ever.

The worst is Aunt Olive though. She's Daddy Wayne's older sister. When she comes I'm not allowed to wear shorts or pants even if they are baggy, only dresses with long sleeves for modesty. She is so holy that no church can keep her. She changes to a different one every time she gets mad at the preacher. She calls the preachers "Brother Bob" or "Brother Jim" and talks about each one like he's a miracle until the next thing you know she has gone to another church with her money. One church named its Bible camp after her but when she left they changed it back to Camp Esther, after the preacher's mother.

Aunt Olive herself preaches. She sets us up in chairs in

the living room and starts in about the Devil. She yells that he is in our house because we are Sinners and Unclean and Overly Proud. We just sit. If you make noises like you agree with her, she says Hippocrit! You just have to wait. It can be a few minutes or it can be an hour. My stomach gets to hurting worse than usual. Then she says Praise the Lord! and it's over for another year.

A secret I know about Aunt Olive is that she has thick silver hair that goes all the way down past her waist. She keeps it tight in a bun with a gray hairnet on top so you never would know, but I saw it once when I forgot she was in my room and I walked in without knocking. She was brushing it like she knew exactly how beautiful it was.

Aunt Olive says: When I pass on to the Lord, don't expect another dime from me. I'm giving you all I'm going to give while I'm alive. I want to watch you all enjoy it. Her idea of enjoying it is different from mine. She makes us turn off lights and wash our dishes in cold water to save every penny. But she won't be here for harvest this year because she is visiting the Holy Land.

She is the opposite of Daddy and Nanny Wayne, who only want us to enjoy their money after they are dead. They'll be here once harvest gets going. Last night I heard Daddy tell Mother he is going to ask Daddy

Wayne for more money again, a bigger part of the crop. He said we will need it for the new baby. Mother said no. She doesn't want her daddy mad. Daddy said Dammit it isn't right to work this hard and be this poor. Mother said You are not thinking ahead very well, Bill Campbell. You'll have all you need once Daddy Wayne dies.

I have heard Daddy Wayne say that exact same thing. He skinnies his eyes up and the words come out like a dare.

Sunday, June 26, 1960

Three of the Wheaties went in to church this morning because they had nothing better to do with their time. One had black hair, one brown and one reddish. All of them are as tall as Daddy. They sat in the back on the row where Alva sits. Everybody in church was trying not to look. The one with black hair sang the hymns loud and sounded better than the preacher.

Afterwards when we were all standing around outside, the brown-haired one went right up to Alva and said, How's your mama? He looked over to the other two Wheaties and laughed mean. I don't have a mama, Alva said straight out and calm. She said, How's yours? I bet you miss her, don't you.

That is what I like about Alva. She can make a grown man walk away from her if she wants him to.

Riding home from church Aunt Coleda was in the front seat with Daddy and I was in the back between Mother and Will. Will pulled his body away from me and turned his face out toward the wheat the whole ride. He hasn't said a word to me since the spanking. Mother pulled me over to her, cozy.

With all the mud, I am having to write in the barn instead of the field. I have a flashlight with me and I'm sitting between the truck and the wall. It smells like diesel and dirt out here. The concrete is cool on my legs.

To get to the barn I had to walk by where the Wheaties were. The one with black hair was standing in the center of the others. I saw him spit six feet up in the air and catch it right back in his mouth. All the other guys hooted and tried it themselves like it would be easy, but they couldn't do it. One said, Big deal, so Earl can spit. There's higher goals a man could set for himself. They all laughed.

I was thinking of telling them that he sings pretty too, but I'm not allowed. If one of them talked to me first, though, I would answer.

Monday, June 27, 1960

Nanny and Daddy Wayne got here this morning. They drove all night up from their big house in Kerrville. They moved there for retirement when Daddy married Mother and we took over here.

They brought us two bushels of over-ripe peaches and two bolts of fabric on sale, bargains too good to pass up. The peaches are brown and soft and if they aren't canned tonight they'll go to waste, Nanny Wayne said. She always brings Mother work to do in the form of a present.

She also always thinks that more of anything is better. She collects antiques, and in her house fancy old dishes are everywhere. High stacks of flowery plates, white glass baskets with lids shaped like setting hens, big jugs with sunsets painted on. She has a whole room of glass cut to look like diamonds. Upstairs the dishes are piled on all the beds and even in the bathtubs and sinks of the bathrooms. She puts price tags on things but when people come to buy she says, Oh no, I can't sell that one.

Now we have peaches in piles all over the kitchen. The big roasting pan is on the stove with water boiling in it, and we put the peaches in a few at a time for just a minute. When they cool a little, it's my job to slip the skins off. Nanny Wayne cuts the peaches up in slices and then I sprinkle them all over with sugar and lemon juice so they don't turn more brown. I bring up the canning jars and lids from the basement. The rest of it Mother has to do by herself, cooking the peaches in syrup and staralizing all the jars. She will be up most of the night after we have all gone to sleep.

Nanny Wayne is the fattest person I know. The tops of her arms are as big as most people's legs. Her bosoms are too big for a bra so they hang down past her waist and she gets that sour smell from where she sweats under them. She likes to rock me in the big rocking chair but her stomach is so big that she doesn't have a lap. I have to hold on tight around her neck to keep from sliding off.

I have seen advertisements for a home reducing plan where the lady just lies down on a magic couch that shakes her all over and the extra pounds disappear. I think she should try that. I would. Every now and then Mother puts me on diets with just melba toast and hard boiled eggs for a week so I won't get fat like Nanny Wayne. I'm always waiting for it to happen.

Nanny and Daddy Wayne brought my brother and me each one of those paddles that have a rubber ball hooked on with elastic. Neither of us can do it right but we keep trying. Mother says when the elastic breaks it will make a good paddle for spanking. She is not joking.

Nanny and Daddy Wayne are sleeping on the back porch and I've moved to the couch in the living room. It's fancy with shiny gold fabric cushions and a dark wood frame. It was on sale. We keep it covered with plastic for protection. There is nothing comfortable about it.

Tuesday, June 28, 1960

I got to talk to the Wheatie with the black hair, the one who sings and spits. I was out by the bunkhouse picking some ripe cherries and he came over to the windmill to fill up a water bottle.

Them sour or sweet? he said.

Sweetish-sour, I said. You can try one if you want. He came right over and got one out of my bucket.

Sourish-sour! he said. He squished up his face. The only thing sweet anywhere near them cherries is you, he said.

I heard you singing in church, I said.

And I seen you over by the tree with that Mexican girl, he said.

That's Alva Higgins, I said. She's not Mexican. She is the smartest person I know.

He laughed. Well, he said, my name's Earl, and I happen to know yours is Lou Ann. I'm pretty smart myself, see. And you're just plain pretty. It has been a pleasure trying out your cherries.

That's all he said. He put his hand up to touch his hat and then walked back to the trailers. The other Wheaties were standing out there watching. They started making whoo-whoo sounds.

He didn't pay them attention. When he got to his trailer door he turned around and waved to me and then he went right in.

No one has ever talked to me like that.

Wednesday, June 29, 1960

Daddy Wayne calls me Jack Dempsey because I am so strong when he arm rassles me. When I was little he used to let me win, but now I think I'm winning for real. He says Jack! Jack! You're hurting me! He puts my elbow up on a big book so we are even. I don't know who Jack Dempsey is for sure.

Nanny Wayne says Stop it, Wayne! You're making her arms lumpy. No boy likes a girl with muscles.

Daddy Wayne will peel an apple for me to eat any time I ask for it. He peels with his pocket knife. Sometimes he leaves a little on here and there. When I tell him to get it off he says those bits of peel are how I can tell that a craftsman peeled my apple and not some machine that does things perfect.

He peels the peel off in one long piece. Nanny Wayne says throw it over my shoulder and whatever letter it comes out, that is who I will marry. It always comes out S. Sam, Simon, Steve, and Scott are the only names I can think of. There is a man in Bussard named Salamo but I'm not marrying anybody named that. Nanny Wayne says Don't forget nicknames like Skip or Scout or Slap. She says Don't be too picky.

I think you have to decide what's worth being picky about. Mother told me that Nanny Wayne made wedding ring quilts for all her nieces when they got married. I said, Did she make one for you? Mother said she was working on it but Daddy Wayne came in one day and cut the quilt right out of the frame. He said he was tired of her having the quilting mess in the living room. Daddy Wayne is fun to be with but I never forget what he did to Nanny Wayne's quilt.

I have to take things like that from my mother but I will be picky about them in the future, when I am grown up.

Now Nanny Wayne is cutting out pajamas and shirts

and dresses for all of us out of the sale fabric she brought with her. One bolt is blue checkered and one is red stripes. She cuts without a pattern and sews things up even faster than Mother. She says with kids it doesn't matter what size you make, they'll grow into it sooner or later.

I like all of us having matching things to wear. I wish we knew how to do acrobatics together or sing all in harmony so we could go on TV as a big famous family.

Aunt Coleda won't wear anything Nanny Wayne makes. She says if we had a sense of fashion, we wouldn't either. Nanny Wayne says fashion, smashion.

I got Nanny Wayne to make me five tiny shirts. I showed her how little I needed them to be and she said, Are you sure these aren't for mice? I didn't tell her they were for the box children. They are part of my family too.

Thursday, June 30, 1960

By the front porch is a tree with the sweetest, juiciest white peaches anybody has ever tasted. The peaches are small and there are never very many. They get ripe the same time as the wheat. I check them every day because we don't want a single one to fall on the ground. To see if a peach is ready, I hold it in my hand and rock it a little. When it's time, the stem lets go easy. We don't make cobbler or jelly out of these peaches. We eat them fresh off the tree. If someone we really like comes to visit, we might give them one or two. Sometimes we think people come to visit around the time of ripe peaches just to get one of our special ones.

I gave one to the Wheatie named Earl.

Yesterday when I went out to the barn to write, I took a peach with me for afterwards. When I came out from writing, Earl was standing by the barn door smoking. He said, I saw you go in there. Kind of a dirty old place for such a pretty girl.

I said, I had some work to do.

Ain't it kind of dark in there? he said.

That's why I have this flashlight, I said.

Is that there peach any sweeter than your cherries was? he said.

It's sweeter than anything, I said. And then I handed it to him. I said, Don't tell anybody I gave you this. They're only for family and good friends.

It's our secret, he said, and besides, we could be good friends. He winked one of his eyes and smiled with all his teeth.

On the way back to the house I was thinking about my reputation. How maybe even just giving a peach to a Wheatie could ruin it. Up till now only men who are friends of Daddy's have ever winked at me. With them it always means a trick.

I picked myself another peach and while I was eating it on the front porch steps I thought about how Earl might be eating his right then too.

Anyway, this morning harvest finally started in the field where the ground is so high it dries out first. Right now they're taking a load of wheat in to test. If it comes out dry enough, we're in business.

Friday, July 1, 1960

Now things are getting exciting. Everyone around is all working for the same thing. Trucks full of wheat head down the road for town every few hours. The Wheaties are on two shifts to keep things moving all the time. I saw Earl go out this morning, so he'll be coming in before suppertime. They don't come in for lunch because Viola Cumberland makes them enough sandwiches for all day. She also gives them big thermos jugs full of hot coffee.

Mother's and my work is different during harvest too because the regular hired hands are off. This gives us a chance to get ready for the 4th of July. We clean the whole house and cook everything we can ahead of time. Nanny Wayne helps some but Aunt Coleda just sits on the front porch smoking and sneaking sips of her liquor that she thinks we don't know about. She is not much of a homemaker.

One thing we do ahead is freeze up ice in empty half-gallon milk cartons. We've been saving the cartons all year and now when we fill them with water and put them in the deep freeze, we'll have enough ice to put the beer in and also for making banana ice cream. We put all the frozen cartons in a gunny sack and whack them over and over with a sledge hammer. Then we pick out the scraps of carton from the crushed ice. You'd be surprised how well this works.

My cleaning jobs are to sweep, mop, wax, and polish all the floors, shine up all the bathroom fixtures, and wash down the porches. My cooking jobs are to make one hundred chocolate chip cookies, peel twenty big potatoes for the potato salad, and mash up all the ingredients for sixty deviled eggs, which Mother says have nothing at all to do with the devil or else we wouldn't eat them.

To keep things fun I pretend I'm in different contests. Who can sweep the floor with the least strokes? Who can squeeze out the mop the driest? Who can polish the floor the shiniest just by dancing around on the polishing rag with their feet? Potato-peeling contests are good too. One is Who can peel by going around the potato in a spiral and leaving the peeling all in one piece like Daddy Wayne does with the apples? Another is Who can peel

fastest with those short choppy hacks downward? Or
Who can make the best faces or diamond shapes on the
potato? I am all the people in all the contests and I am
also the judges. I always win.

On the actual day of July 4th we will still have lots of
last minute things to do, like mixing up the fruit soda
punch for the kids. When we serve it, we put a scoop of
orange or lime sherbert right in each cup. The kids get
to pick whichever flavor they want. We shape up all the
hamburger patties for Daddy to bar-be-que. He likes
them bigger than the buns and not too thick. We cut up
tomatoes, onions, lettuce and pickles, all from the garden. We cover it all over with tinfoil so the flies won't
have a meal.

My brother's job is to mow the weeds that grow
all around the house. When he's done it looks like a
real yard.

Saturday, July 2, 1960

Yesterday after I did all the work I could for one day, I
went out for a little walk around the driveway. I told
Mother I wanted to see the sunset which is true but I was

also thinking maybe I would see Earl too. I did. He was standing around with some of the other men from the early shift and when he saw me he walked right over. Here is what we said.

Him: Hey Lou Ann. How's my favorite pretty girl this evening?

Me: Hi Earl. I'm fine thank you. How come you keep on saying things about pretty?

Him: You want me to stop?

Me: I don't know. I just don't like teasing. I know about my ankles being fat.

Him: Who told you that?

Me: Daddy.

Him: Well Bill Campbell's a good man but he's a little loose in the head on that one, sweetheart. Everything about you is fine, real fine. You got anything else strange you want to ask about?

Me: I don't guess so. Did you like your peach?

Him: Never had one sweeter! Wish I had another one right now. I'm hungry and dirty and bone tired. I reckon I'll be better after supper and a good night's sleep. You be good now.

Me: Wait. I do have another question. Do I have bad breath?

Him: I ain't never smelled anything but sweetness
    on you.

Me: But you never get right up close to my mouth.

Him: Is this some kind of trick?

Me: No! I just need you to smell my breath. I have rea-
    sons to think it's always bad and I need to know.
    Please?

He shrugged his shoulders and put his nose up to my
mouth while I blew out.

Just like roses, he said. He rolled his eyes and said
Now goodnight, Lou Ann.

Then he walked back to the others.

There are more things I wish I had asked him. Where
does he live most of the time? Does he have a brother or
a sister? Does he tell lots of girls they're pretty? I don't
think he means to tease me. I just think some people
might not care about fat ankles and bad breath the way
Daddy and Mother do. That is good information to have.

I wonder if he knows all the bad things people say
about Wheaties. They say to lock your doors or things
will disappear when Wheaties are around. They say pro-
tect your daughters. They say most Wheaties are running from something, maybe even the law. The only bad
thing I know they do is pee in the weeds.

We won't be done with harvest by the 4th. Almost, but not quite. We have to pay the cutters even if they don't work on the 4th or else they'll leave and go on to the next farmer. They don't just stay out of niceness.

Sunday, July 3, 1960

On the sidewalk in back there are places you can see where we have lit snakes made of ash for the 4th of July in other years. We buy them in red cardboard boxes of ten black pellets that look like magnets. This is the only firework Mother will let me do before the 4th. You have to hold the match over the pellet for a while before it will catch. Then all of a sudden it comes to life, flaming at the base and rising up curly and black, longer and longer. Then it falls over, broken and finished. You can hold the ash in your hand carefully or else crush it to nothing. All that's left is a smudge on your hand and a stain on the concrete.

But my favorites are the sparklers. It takes two people for them, one to hold and one to light. Usually I hold the sparkler steady while my brother holds the match to the tip and we wait. They start by sputtering, then the fire takes hold and the sparks start. I write my name in the air,

Lou Ann. I write my brother's name, Will. I make stars and diamonds and moons and when I know there's not much time I write even faster. I keep writing until no sparks are left and I am standing with a bent black metal wire too hot to touch.

I wonder if Will is still too mad to do sparklers with me?

The one thing I hate is firecrackers. When the Farrell boys came last year they brought lots of them and went around doing bad things. They found a little frog and put it in the hole in the center of a brick, then put in a firecracker and lit it. They laughed when the guts and blood splattered everywhere. They also blew up a bird egg, an apricot from our tree, and a Coke bottle. Bombs away! they said. The other girls were afraid to look, but I followed them around to every new explosion.

Tomorrow morning Daddy and Duke Yakes will drive our pickup over the Oklahoma line and fill up the back with beer. Sometimes it's after lunch before they come back and they're already drunk. Daddy can handle it but Duke is another story. Last year he put on his swimsuit and climbed up the metal ladder on the windmill yelling King of the Mountain! He wobbled out onto the new diving board Daddy built up there and crashed down into the tank water on his belly. The tank was so full that water poured over the sides in a big wave when he hit.

Then he pulled himself up out of the water where there isn't a ladder and thumped down onto the concrete sidewalk below. It's a ten-foot fall, but Duke stumbled right up laughing and walked off crooked to get himself another beer.

Daddy and Duke will put the beer in three big metal tubs with the busted-up milk carton ice. Then they'll settle down in front of the water cooler on the back porch and start sit-down drinking while they wait for everybody else to come about 3 or 4. Sometimes Aunt Coleda will come out and sit with them. Nanny Wayne will help Mother, and Daddy Wayne will stay in the bedroom listening to the radio. He doesn't like parties.

The same people will come that always come. Mack and Rinnie Roker with their three red-headed girls, Rona, Carla, and Betsy, who's my best friend during school; Dean and Maydean Cooper and their little girl Deana who is only four; Jess and Helen Farrell with their three rough boys, Brick, James, and Wiley; Duke (the one that comes early to drink with Daddy) and Fran Yakes with their five kids, Conny, Ronny, Lonny, Bonny, and Walterine (she's named after her granddaddy); and Key and Mavie Garner with their girl Royal Jean. Mavie's hair is dyed yellow-white. She wears shortshorts and tops that look like bras with flowers on them. She plays the Hokey

Pokey on the piano and we all put our right feet in and put our right feet out. She plays by ear and Mother says every song sounds exactly the same.

All together with my brother and me there will be fifteen kids here. Rona Roker is the oldest, sixteen, and she doesn't like to play much any more. She will bring a book to read. Next comes the Farrell boys and Conny Yakes, then my brother, then me, Betsy Roker, and Ronny Yakes. All the rest are younger all the way down to Deana but we will play with them anyway.

I think Brick Farrell is cute but he thinks I talk too much, he told my brother so. He likes to jump off the diving board holding his knees in a cannonball to splash the rest of us. When I go up on the board with everyone watching, I get scared and most of the time I end up doing a belly buster like Duke Yakes. If you're not drunk, it hurts.

After swimming we'll play Swing the Statue, Red Rover Red Rover, and Kick the Can. No one will leave until way after dark, after the grand fireworks. We'll have bottle rockets, screaming swizzlers, and roman candles with seven rounds that bust full against the sky.

It makes me proud that all these people come out to our house every year for the 4th of July. It's the greatest day of summer.

It's late and I am writing with a flashlight under the covers. The grownups are all asleep after lots of drinking so I think I'm safe.

Today was not what I expected. I don't know how things will ever get back to the same as before.

First of all, my brother would not play with me at all. He wouldn't do snakes or sparklers. He wouldn't be on any team I was on. I sat down next to him when he was eating his hamburger to say I'm sorry I ever asked Mother about fuckin, but he just picked up his plate and went to sit on the back steps. I started to follow him but he said Go play with your little girl friends.

In the swimming tank the Farrell boys kept dunking me and trying to feel around on me with their hands. They pretended to be tickling but I know the difference.

Then when I was waiting on the back porch for Betsy Roker to come out of the bathroom, Brick Farrell came up behind me and put his hand over my mouth tight. He jerked me around toward him and then put his mouth on mine and started pushing and swirling his tongue all around. When he heard Betsy opening the door he let go and walked off like nothing happened. Betsy came out and said When you get done, can we play Tom and Sue?

I couldn't get any words to come out so I just shook my head No. I stayed in the bathroom and splashed water on my face a long time.

After all that I went out to the wheat bin because I needed some peace and quiet. I was on top of the wheat sitting with my legs crossed down into it when I heard Daddy's voice. He knows I come there but he didn't know I was there then.

What he said was, This is the best idea I've had all day. Then a lady's voice said, I doubt that, Bill, I imagine a smart guy like you gets lots of good ideas. She laughed loud and I could tell it was Mavie Garner in her short-shorts.

Next I heard them walking right past the bin I was in and then all I heard was mmm and amm sounds like when you've just had a big bite of really good ice cream and you're licking the extra off the outside of your mouth. That went on for a while. I know because I was being still and you can feel time going by in all its seconds if nothing else is moving.

Then Mavie's voice all thick said Hey darlin, if you're not gonna finish me off I think we better get on back because I am reaching the point of no return here.

Then Daddy's voice said, I could kiss you all day. And Mavie said, Well I was hoping we'd get on to other things, big boy. Daddy said, I'll have to take a rain check on that, sweetheart, or Loretta's gonna get ideas again. And Mavie said, It don't rain around here nearly often enough, Bill.

Then they started walking away. When I heard their foot sounds change from concrete to dirt I knew they were out of the barn and I climbed up out of the wheat bin to see what would happen next. From the edge of the barn door I watched the two of them walk straight back toward the house like they had just been out to look at a new plow. I saw Mother and Nanny Wayne standing at the back porch window looking right at them. Nobody saw me.

Daddy headed over to where the men were talking and Mavie climbed up the ladder to the swimming tank. All the men including Daddy watched her legs while she was climbing. When she got to the wooden platform at the top, she sat down sideways like the ladies in the pinup pictures. She waved and the men laughed big.

Mother came out carrying the ice cream freezer, which she is not supposed to do because of the baby. Daddy saw her and ran over. He said What are you doing Loretta? Mother said really loud, I thought maybe somebody out here could help me get this banana ice cream hard. It's no use to anybody all soft, is it. Mavie, maybe you could come down here and crank awhile. I know you don't give up until you get a firm result.

Mavie laughed and said, Get Bill to help you. He's always good for a quick turn or two.

Mother stood looking at everybody that was looking at her. She put a big smile on her face and said, I have an announcement to make. Bill and I are going to have another baby. Isn't that wonderful? I'm four months along. Bill is so proud he wanted to tell right away but I said let's wait for the right moment.

Daddy lit into turning the ice cream crank. He was looking down with his face all red. Everybody started cheering and saying things like Bill, you son of a gun! Speech, speech!

There is a way Daddy can look that is worse than mad. If you know him, you know to just stay out of the way. He kept churning with that face and didn't say a word.

The ladies, all except Mavie, came and stood around Mother and said When are you due and Do you want a boy or a girl? Mother said A boy but we will take whatever we get. Rinnie Roker asked, Have you had any trouble? Mother said, Not a day of it.

She made her face look as happy as I have ever seen it.

As for me I'm all turned around inside my head. I can't even get myself to cry.

Today is worse than yesterday.

I woke up late on the lumpy old couch and heard Daddy talking on the front porch with Daddy Wayne about settling up with the cutters. They'll have to be paid when they finish up tomorrow, and Daddy and Nanny Wayne will already be gone.

Daddy explained how it will cost more than usual because of the rain and having to pay the cutters for July 4. Daddy Wayne is the one who pays them and he said he wasn't shelling out a dime for a day of drinking and fooling around with other people's wives. He said Daddy did not have his pryortees straight and that nothing comes before getting the wheat in. He said he is taking the July 4th money for the cutters out of the share Daddy is getting from the harvest.

Daddy blew up over that. I have never heard him yell at Daddy Wayne before but he did it today. He said he's already going broke trying to make a living. He said he might as well be a slave. He said his idea of fair was to ask for more money this year, and here Daddy Wayne was talking less.

Daddy Wayne kept his voice low but you could hear everything he said clear as crystal.

DW: Bill, let me ask you some questions. Who gave
    you the tractors and plows you farm with?

Daddy: You did.

DW: You did what?

Daddy: You did, sir.

DW: And who gave you the house you live in?

Daddy: You did sir and I'm very grateful it's just

DW: Who bought you your pickup truck?

Daddy: You did sir.

DW: And who did I let marry my youngest daughter
    even though he came from white trash?

Daddy didn't say anything.

DW: You, that's who. And the reason I did that was
    because I thought you would be a good worker
    and I thought you would remember your place.
    But you watch your step now, Bill Campbell.
    There's other men who'd love to farm this land,
    and we can always take care of Loretta if it comes
    to that. I think you need a little reminder about
    what comes first. Harvest comes first. Your own
    wife comes first. Whatever I say comes first comes
    first. Now maybe after you've shown me that you
    understand about all this, maybe then I will bring

up the subject of how much money you think you
have coming to you.

Then Daddy Wayne wrote out a check for the cutters
and a check for Daddy. He said, If you don't like this
amount, I can keep it. He held it out and made Daddy
reach for it.

Nanny Wayne was loading up their car while all this
was going on like she didn't know a thing about it.
Mother was looking out the window with her hands in
her lap and a little smile.

My stomach has been hurting all day but I'm not saying anything because I don't want any medicine. All I
want is for Aunt Coleda to leave too so the box children
and I can have our room back.

Wednesday, July 6, 1960

Last night after everyone went to bed I couldn't sleep
so I went out on the front porch and watched the com-
bine lights on the field in front of the house, the last one
left to cut.

Then I went over to the side of the porch and saw Earl
washing off his face at the windmill. I jumped off the

porch and ran over there. I didn't even think about it before I did it.

Here is what we said.

Him: Hey Lou Ann. Ain't it past your bedtime?

Me: I wanted to say bye because harvest will be over
after tonight and you all will be gone in the morning after the settling up.

Him: That's special of you. I appreciate that. I really do.

He stood just looking at me for a minute. That's when
I remembered I was in my nightgown. I crossed my arms
over my chest.

Him: How old are you, Lou Ann?

Me: 11. How old are you?

Him: Well I'm 20 with a birthday coming up in August. If you was a little older I'd ask you if you
wanted a goodbye kiss but I think I better wait a
few years on that, what do you say?

Me: I don't know. I'll be twelve in ten days.

Him: Have you ever had a kiss?

I didn't know what to say. I think what Brick did would
count as something but I am hoping it was not a kiss.

Not one I wanted, is what I said.

Him: Well, I don't know. Maybe next summer if I
come back through we could see about it then.
Me: We could see about it now if you want.
Him: OOO boy. You got no idea what you're dealing
with, sweetheart. Come on over here.

So I did.

He bent down and smooched his lips soft on my fore-
head, right where my bangs are, and then he turned his
head to the side and pointed on his cheek. Now gimme
one right here, he said.

So I did. Then he put his finger under my chin and
said, Now you go on back to bed and be glad my mama
raised me right. And don't be going out at night like
this, it ain't safe. Although I am glad you did it just this
one time.

Me too, I said. Then I ran back to the porch. When I
turned and looked he was still standing by the windmill
but he didn't wave.

I can still feel the way his cheek was on my mouth,
cool and smooth but with a little bit of whiskers.

Thursday, July 7, 1960

I was right about the cutters finishing up and leaving. They were gone this morning. Aunt Coleda finally left too so I have my room back. But it stinks. It will be days before the perfume, liquor, and cigarette-smoke smell is out of there. I wish I had masks for the box children. They hate smoke.

It's strange to have things be so still after all the excitement. We are back to our regular days and my brother and Daddy and the hired hands have already started plowing under all the wheat stubble. It makes me sad to see the half-stalks sticking up out there. I think about the roots, how hard they worked all year to hold everything together and draw in whatever the rest of the plant needed to grow. After harvest, roots don't matter at all.

I'm writing laying down flat in a ditch a little ways down the road from our house. I wanted to get as much away as I could for today.

I feel tight where my heart is. I keep thinking about Daddy kissing Mavie, and about Brick doing what he did, and about my brother, who acts like I am not even here. I worry too about the new baby, now that Mother has announced it to the world. What is it doing right this minute? Is it OK? There is no way for me to know.

Thinking about Earl is the only thing that helps. I want him to be out there every night for me to talk to and give a kiss. I haven't liked anything in my life so far as much as that.

As soon as I finish writing I plan to go out in the stubble to sing. It helps me sometimes. No one can hear if I go out far enough. My songs are Autumn Leaves, Green Fields, and The Wayward Wind. I sing the same ones over and over.

I want to write to Wyn Rue about Earl and all the things that have happened. Mother would never let me, but I'm thinking maybe there's a way to get past her. I could write a nice fake letter, and after Mother reads it and gives me the stamp I could stick the real one in the envelope fast before I seal it all up. I think Penny Coffee would like that idea.

The last letter I got from Wyn said she got a new polka-dotted swim suit with ruffles on the back to wear to the Country Club for the 4th of July. They have a big swimming pool there, the kind with the blue-painted bottom and the rope going across to separate the deep from the shallow. She said our swimming tank sounds better because we can swim any time and only invite who we want. She said last year two high school boys played catch with her in the water and it wasn't as much fun as it might sound.

Since the 4th of July, Mother has been being nicey-nice to Daddy. She asks him if he wants more ice in his tea dear. She asks the hired hands do they know how lucky they are to be working for such a great farmer as Bill Campbell. Lonnie Helfenbein is the only one who doesn't know she is being mean. He says I do know that, Ma'am.

I have noticed that Lonnie always thinks the best of people. I think it helps Daddy to have him around. I like him too.

Friday, July 8, 1960

Today for lunch we cooked chicken fried steak and gravy with mashed potatoes. This is usually one of the favorite meals but today it was not. Here is why: first of all Mother told me not to pound the steak. If you don't pound the steak, it's too tough to eat. But with the fried batter on it, you can't tell that by looking. You just bite into it and then chew forever.

She only had me pound two pieces tender, one for her and one for me, and she kept them over to the side.

Then while she was making the gravy she said, Watch this. She held the pepper box over the skillet and kept shaking and shaking it. Say WHEN! she said. I said When but she kept on shaking and laughing like a witch.

After the potatoes were all mashed I saw her take the horseradish out of the refrigerator and put in three big spoonfuls. She looked over at me and said, Your Daddy likes things spicy these days. Then she said Don't worry, I took some potatoes out for us.

She rang the dinner bell and called out, Come and Get It! Daddy says people are like dogs and the salava in their mouths gets going just from hearing the bell. I wished there was a way to ring it that would say, Don't get your mouth too worked up, dinner is strange today.

I watched Daddy load up his plate and dig in. He likes to eat bites with a little bit of everything in them, so he got a big firey mouthful for sure. He spit it right back out on the plate. He yelled Goddammit Loretta what are you trying to do here?

There is no need to take The Lord's name in vain, Mother said all sweet. I just thought maybe you needed a little more excitement in your life and a little more exercise for your mouth. You seem to think you haven't been getting enough.

Oh for Christ sake, Daddy said. Don't bring trouble

into the food. I said I was sorry. Now where's the real dinner? We can't eat this.

Eat it or wear it, Mother said. Makes no difference to me. Then she went off into their bedroom and slammed the door.

Daddy told me to bring out extra bread and some peanut butter and jelly and we had sandwiches. He told the hired hands, I'm sorry about the way my wife is acting. If you ever get married you'll have times like this. There's no accounting for what a woman will do.

I found some raisins and chocolate chips and mixed them up for a special dessert. I don't think the hired hands should have to be hungry because of somebody else's fight. I do think there is some accounting for what Mother is doing, and I think Daddy knows exactly what the numbers add up to.

After I cleared the table and threw away all the food the men didn't eat, Mother came in and got out the dinner she had set aside for her and me.

I told her I was already full.

She said, Aren't you Miss Smartypants. Next time if I were you I'd eat with the one who cooked for you. In fact, I'm not sure that the food you ate counts at all. Sit on down here and eat your dinner.

There has never been a time Mother has ever told me

to eat more. I asked her what about getting fat like Nanny Wayne and she said, Do what I tell you.

She had me eat until I was nearly sick. You can't be on both sides in a war, she said.

She scrubbed me harder than ever in the bath.

Saturday, July 9, 1960

Now that the wheat is gone, my new writing place is underneath the last cherry tree by the side of the bunkhouse. There's a row of six of them and this last one has really low branches. To see me, you'd have to be standing in the tomatoes, which only the person watering or picking them ever does. And usually that is me. I like being here in the shade and I like looking out at the road and fields.

To keep my mind off of everything I'm going to write about some of the things I'm afraid of around here.

One is rattlesnakes. They like to hide under things and they like it where it's dry. We have found them in our woodpile when that wasn't what we were looking for. It's the kind of surprise you never want. Once we found a mother and her babies that had just hatched, all wiggly. Daddy chopped them up with a hoe. After a rain rattlesnakes come out of the ditches onto the road and Daddy runs over them fast forward and backward several times. He keeps a hoe in the trunk for making sure they're dead after they don't move any more. If one bites you, you should cut an X in your arm or leg or wherever the bite is and suck out the poison. Otherwise you'll die. Then spit the poison out so you won't get sick.

Also black widows. They're a kind of spider that has an hour-glass shape on their stomachs. They can kill you too. Sometimes I get closer to a spider than I should just to see if it's a black widow. I like to know whether to be scared or not. Even if it is, I don't kill them. I'm always afraid that somehow they'll get me back, or that their children or friends will come after me or the box children at night when we're asleep. It's better to just go play somewhere else.

Another thing is yellow jackets and purple wasps. They make nests under where the roof hangs over, and also in the cherry tree branches. For most people their bite only hurts a lot, but for me it's more dangerous. I have built up an allergy from being bit every single summer while I'm out picking cherries. Last summer the place behind my knee swoll up so much I couldn't walk. Dr. Healey gave us some shot needles and some medicine we keep in the refrigerator for when it happens again. After I get bit, Daddy goes out looking for the nest and splashes gasoline up all over it. The wasps swarm out and then drop to the ground dead.

Chiggers are not something I'm afraid of exactly but I sure do hate getting them. They are tiny red bugs that like to crawl in all under your clothes but most especially under the elastic in your underpants. They eat right into your skin and then they stay there itching you like mad. Nothing itches worse. They like elastic because it keeps scratching them and that gives them air so they can stay alive in there. I've had a hundred of them at a time. We paint over them with clear nail polish to close off the air. Even with that it takes a few days for them to give up and die. People have them in their yards if they don't spray once in a while. You can get them bad playing Swing the Statue.

Some things I am afraid of I'm not even sure are real. For example there's a poem Daddy reads to us about Little Orphant Annie that gives me bad dreams. The part that scares me the most is:

> *Once there was a little girl who'd always laugh and grin*
> *And make fun of everyone and all her blood and kin*
> *And once when there was company and old folks was*
> *   there*

She mocked 'em and she shocked 'em and she said she
    didn't care.
And just as she had kicked her heels and turned to run
    and hide
There was two great big old black things a' standing by
    her side
And they snatched her through the ceiling 'fore she
    knowed what she's about
And the goblins will get YOU, if you don't watch out.

I worry about that little girl. What happened to her after that? Does she have to live with the great big old black things now? Will she ever come back?

I hope I never get snatched up through the ceiling. I would rather be bit by a rattlesnake any day.

Sunday, July 10, 1960

Yesterday afternoon we went over to Wheatly instead of just into Bussard, just me and Mother. My brother never wants to come with us any more. I told him I'd get the new Supermans for him but he acted like he didn't even hear me.

Mother went to a store we never go to where they

have lots of flowers. She bought whole bunches of big plastic ones, yellow, blue, red, pink, orange, purple and white, every color they had. She bought five big orange vases. It was probably the most anybody had ever bought from that store at one time. The store lady said, Having a party?

Life's a party, Mother said.

Then she said, My husband wants a little more excitement in our home. Also, a new baby is on the way and I've heard they love color.

All the time Mother was picking out the flowers I was thinking how she usually says the devil loves decoration. I have always wondered how she fits that idea with the flowers she embroiders on my dresses. Maybe flowers don't count as decoration since they are nature.

I was also wondering about money. I didn't think we had enough to be spending it on plastic flowers. But in the car Mother said, Is there anything you want special? Nanny Wayne is making sure us girls have what we need to make up for everything. I can get you anything you want at all.

Could I get a storebought dress? I said.

You never stop being ungrateful, do you? she said. Think of something else.

Could I get a spiral notebook? I said.

What do you need with a spiral notebook? she said. Pick something nice like a little necklace or some dressup shoes. Whatever you want.

I don't guess I want anything, I said. But thank you all the same.

Listen to her pretend she has manners, Mother said. Aren't you the one. Do you think your Daddy will like these flowers?

Not very much, I said. I think he likes things plain.

Well. Your plain old Daddy has been doing some fancy things, she said. Do you know anything about that?

No ma'am, I said. There was no reason I could see to tell the truth.

Well let's just say he has shown a liking for things beyond what a Christian woman would normally provide in her home. So I am giving him some little reminders that there are surprises on all sides once you turn off the road of the righteous, she said.

You can learn a lot from this, she said.

After that we went to the food store. We hardly bought any of what we usually get. Instead we got big boxes of instant mashed potatoes, cans of vienna sausages, and cans of spaghetti with meatballs. Daddy hates spaghetti with meatballs. We got whole wheat bread instead of white. We got canned spinach and canned peas and canned chili with beans. Mother said she has plenty of good food for the two of us and that the men will just have to eat what she puts in front of them. She says anyway it will be a balanced diet.

The grocery bag boy was there at the checkout line. He said Hi Penny! Mother turned around and smiled big at me because now she has made me have a secret with her against the boy. I didn't know that would happen.

He had to put the groceries in the back seat because the flowers and vases had already filled up the trunk. When we drove off I didn't even wave with my finger. I don't see the purpose any more. He thinks he's waving at someone named Penny.

Monday, July 11, 1960

Now we have big orange vases of plastic flowers all over the house. One is on the back porch table just as you come in, one is in the middle of the table where we eat, one is on the chester drawers in Mother and Daddy's bedroom, one is in the bathroom on top of the bin where we keep bathing suits, and one is on the table right in the middle of the living room. If you walked into our house for the first time, the flowers are all you would notice.

When Daddy saw them he said For God sake Loretta, how much did all these cost?

Less than your mistakes, Mother said.

At the dinner table we have to reach around the flowers to pass the food. We can't see who is across the table from us. I think Daddy must have told my brother and the hired hands not to say anything about them because I am pretty sure somebody would have otherwise. Just to be nice Lonnie might have even said they were pretty, which they are not. But even he is keeping quiet. So everyone at the table is putting their attention into not paying attention to the flowers.

That and the food they are eating. Which today is instant mashed potatoes mixed with ketchup, chili, and spinach. At least there's plenty of it. Mother and I just sit and pretend to eat, then have the real meal after.

I'm starting to make Mother a top to wear when she gets bigger from the baby. It's the first sewing I have ever done for a grownup. In Wheatly Mother picked out material with diamond shapes of dark green, light green, dark pink and light pink. She picked out a Simplicity pattern that is not simple at all. First I pinned all the pattern pieces to the material, then I cut them out with Mother's good pinking shears. One thing I don't understand is why the cutting line is printed solid on the pattern, and the seam line is dotted. I would do it the other way around.

Mother says she will let me use the sewing machine for three days and that should be enough. She says to hurry up so she can wear her beautiful new maternity blouse. That's what she calls it.

I took a piece of the fabric to show to the box children. They don't like it. They say the diamond shapes are too sharp for a baby. Babies like round soft things, they say.

I told them Mother did the choosing.

Tuesday, July 12, 1960

While I am making the maternity blouse, Mother is going all around the house deciding what's wrong with things. She says we need curtains and some exciting pictures on the walls. New lamps. She walks from room to room with a sharp pencil and her list. Her eyes shine like in a scary movie.

And of course there is the refrigerator. Today she cut out a picture of one with the features she wants and pasted it right on the front of our old refrigerator. If I had done that I would get hit for sure. I do like the one she picked out though. It's pale blue-green. We would have to paint the kitchen to match but she has probably already thought of that.

The sewing is going OK. But if I need help there's no one to ask for it. When I ask Mother she says If I am going to have to tell you how to do every little thing, I'd just as soon do it myself.

So I read the instructions over and over and then I pin everything together before I sew it. That way I can picture how it will be. Even then sometimes it comes out wrong and I have to take out the stitches and start all over. When I sew the seam it feels good that every stitch is closer to the end. Then I cut the threads and hold it up to see how it looks. When it's right I can feel how sewing could be a pleasure for some people.

Here is what I think about while I work on the blouse: I want the baby to know that somebody out here already cares about it enough to make something special for it. I want the baby to know that if there's something about Mother that makes being born seem like it might not be a good idea, I am right here to help. And if there's something wrong with the baby, I want it to know I've already started being sad about that. There's nothing else I can do for now.

Doing the sewing doesn't mean I don't have to do my other chores. The refrigerator, the trash, the bathroom, mopping the kitchen floor. Cooking the meals takes twice as long now because we're fixing strange things for them and good things for us. Mother has also decided that there's too much dust in the corners of things and that I need to take care of that. She says part of what happened with Daddy is her fault because she has not been vigilant against filth. She got some new spray that you put on a rag and after supper I go around dust hunting. You would not imagine how much dust can creep inside a house when you live in the middle of a field.

Before I did this writing, I started on my long letter to Wyn Rue, the one I really plan to send her. It's the first time I have ever tried to tell real things to an outside person. I got to feeling nervous, a lot more than just writing this diary, which I wrote her about. I also wrote about my brother, about Earl, and about the new baby. I'm writing in small letters and using the front and back of the pages. I think Wyn will be glad I have more exciting things to tell than just about cleaning house.

Wednesday, July 13, 1960

I am going to write what happened yesterday from start to finish even though all I am thinking about right now is the ending and what I should have done different.

Daddy was gone all yesterday afternoon. He didn't even come home for supper. I told Mother he probably had a flat tire or ran out of gas. Or maybe he got somewhere and something happened and they didn't have a phone so he couldn't tell us what he was doing.

She said Well little miss Pollyanna, you just can't stand to think a bad thought about that Daddy of yours, can you? She told me to go to my room and shut the door behind me because she couldn't stand my cheery face another second. She gave me a coathanger to braid, to keep me busy.

Usually she likes me cheery but not last night.

Daddy got home after ten. I could tell from his voice he was drunk, which never happens on a week night.

I heard Mother say You are not coming into this bedroom Bill Campbell. And if you ever come home late and drunk like this again I will not even let you in my house. Some father you are. I must be crazy bringing a new baby into this mess.

I had just finished braiding the hanger and putting on my shorty pajamas when Daddy turned my door handle and poked his head in. Can I come say nighty night? he said real quiet. He never tells me goodnight usually. He had a big bruise on his cheek.

He sat down on my bed and just stared at me. I was standing by my dresser with my arms crossed.

If I wasn't your Daddy I'd say you look real sexy, he said. What do you think of that?

I didn't say anything.

Come on over here and sit on my lap for a ride, he said. He used his gruff voice.

I went.

Trotta Ma Horse and GO TO TOWN! he said. On the loud words he pounded his boot on the floor and grabbed me tight under my arms. My pajama top is kind of loose so his hand went inside by accident.

Instead of getting tired and telling me that's enough he kept on going. His hands slid all over my front.

He finally stopped but his hands stayed under my arms and he picked me up high and threw me on the bed with a bounce. Here comes Tickle Mouse! he said. I used to like that game but I think now I am too old for it.

So I said, Mother said it's past my bedtime. I rolled off the bed to the other side and grabbed hold of the pillow to put in front of me.

Daddy looked around then like he was lost. His face

was all red and the bruise was swelling up. He said You better watch what you wear around here. A man can't help himself.

Then he went out to sleep on the back porch bed.

I got into my own bed and held myself completely still but tears started coming out of my eyes anyway. I squeezed my face tight and held my breath as long as I could but I couldn't help crying. I am not sure why. He was only trying to play.

I was kind of hoping Mother might come in after she heard him in here so loud. Usually after bedtime she doesn't let there be any noise. But she probably would've said it was my own fault anyway.

Maybe she's right. If I had been wearing my regular nightgown nothing would have happened probably. I will know that from now on. I only wore the shorty pajamas because it was such a hot night. I wasn't expecting a visit from my Daddy.

Thursday, July 14, 1960

This morning early Mother left without me in the car. She wrote a note that said I should put out cereal and milk for breakfast and make baloney sandwiches for lunch, three for each man.

When Daddy came in for breakfast his face was still swollen up. He kept his eyes down. The hired hands and my brother didn't say a thing about how he looked. I said I hoped everybody liked their cereal and Lonnie said it seemed real fresh.

After I did the dishes, I finished my real letter to Wyn Rue, and wrote the pretend one to show Mother. I ended up not writing about Daddy and Mavie. I wasn't in the mood I guess.

I had the lunch sandwiches all made up and on the table when Mother drove up. She left the car out by the windmill and got me to help her unload two big heavy boxes. I told her she shouldn't be lifting but she gave me a Shut Up look. She put the boxes on the kitchen counter and when I said What are these? she said You'll see. I was hoping it might have something to do with my birthday, which is only two days away.

After the men came in and started eating, Mother said

Can I have your all's attention please? She said, I have a new set of dishes here I want to show you.

She held up a plate with pink flowers all over it and silver around the edges. She held up a cup, a saucer, and a bowl. Then she held up a big platter and a gravy boat, all with the same decoration.

Daddy watched her do all that and then said real quiet, Those are nice dishes Loretta but we already have a whole bunch of things to eat off of, don't we?

Mother smiled like that was just the question she was waiting for. She reached into the cabinet and pulled out two of our old plates. She held them up, one in each hand.

You mean these? she said. And then she crashed them into the sink. She took out two more and did the same, then two more. I have put up with these plain old ugly plates for long enough, she yelled. Some people around here do exactly what they want all the time and I am going to do the same from now on!

She took her arm and wiped the whole shelf of our old cups and saucers to the floor. Not all of them broke because they are thick Navy surplus. The ones that didn't break she picked up and threw at the wall. She almost hit Daddy.

It happened faster than I am telling it. When two

whole shelves were empty the yelling turned to loud cry-talking. She said Bill Campbell does not even love me enough to come home at night for supper. I try and I try to make a good home but I don't know how much more of this I can take.

She finally just sat down on the floor crying in the middle of the broken dishes.

Up until then Daddy was watching like she was a movie. Now he got up and went over to put his arms around her. At first she said Don't touch me! But he kept holding on and after a while she started holding him back, then they both were cry-talking soft.

Daddy promised he would never hurt her again. He said he knew how much he had to be thankful for and he would do his best to make a good life for her and the new baby.

I guess me and my brother will have to make a good life for ourselves.

Daddy asked Mother what she would like to do next. She said she needed to rest. He got her a beer and walked her back to their bedroom. Then he came into the kitchen and said Let's all clean this mess up. So we did that. My brother and Les and Buck picked up the big pieces of glass. Lonnie held the dustpan while I swept in all the little bits. Daddy unpacked the new dishes into the cabinet.

When they were finished and walking out I heard Daddy say to the hired hands, That should do it. Sometimes you have to just say whatever it takes to make a woman happy.

Maybe now things will settle down.

Friday, July 15, 1960

I finished the maternity blouse yesterday. I forgot how long it takes to hem things with those little invisible stitches. For my dolls I just leave the edges raggedy, but for Mother it had to be perfect.

She put the blouse on the minute it was done and she has it on again today. She wants to wear it into Bussard to the grocery store tomorrow. She wants me to make her another one out of the same Simplicity pattern.

I said I would if she would let me pick out the material. I want to get colors and shapes the baby will like better. Something with pale blue like the sky would be good. Something to let the baby know what all is possible out here.

I got up the nerve to remind Mother that tomorrow is my birthday just in case she might have forgotten, and she said What kind of a mother would forget the day her only daughter came into God's world?

Since she was in such a good mood, I also showed her the pretend letter to Wyn Rue. She said it was a very nice letter and she gave me a stamp for the envelope. Then I put the real letter in, sealed it up, and put it in the mailbox to start its trip to Oklahoma City.

Today we fixed normal food and everybody seemed happy about that. Mother even took the big orange vase off the kitchen table.

But it is strange to eat off of flowery dishes when you never have. I am afraid some will break when we wash and dry them because they are so thin. I hope I'm not the person who breaks the first one. It will ruin the whole set.

It's funny how you get used to things and you never even think they could be different. We had the Navy plates for as long as I have been noticing things. To me they were just our dishes. It never came into my mind that we could break them and get some others. I wonder what all other kinds of dishes there are. Maybe some with wild bright colors, or music notes, or pictures of animals. A person could get whatever they are interested in. Every person in a family could have a different kind of plate if they wanted. You could get a new one every birthday.

Now I am wondering how many other things could be different in a second if I had the push inside myself to throw out all the things I know so well.

Saturday, July 16, 1960

Happy Birthday to Me!

At the grocery store this morning we bought my favorite, a white cake mix and chocolate frosting mix, and a package of all-colored candles. I made the cake and we'll all have it after supper. I bet my brother will be glad about that. He likes cake even more than I do. I'll give him a big piece and maybe he'll say Thank you.

The box children have a surprise party planned for later, but I found out. I'll act surprised anyway because I don't want to spoil their fun.

For my birthday Mother gave me something I have never had before, a bra. She says it's time because I'm getting to be a young lady and that from now on I have to wear it every day. It doesn't really fit but she says I'll grow into it. It's white and has a tiny pink rose on each side where the straps are. I like it a lot. She also gave me seven pairs of underwear from the Sears and Roebuck's catalogue. Each pair has a day of the week stitched in cursive with a heart around it, a different color for each day. She gave them to me because she says I don't change often enough. I think that is my business but she thinks it's hers. I plan to wear the days all out of order just to mix her up. The underwear's pretty, though, and fancier than any I have had before.

She said now that I'm twelve, I need also to pay attention to the fact that my eyebrows are growing in the wrong places. After lunch she sat me down and pulled the bad hairs out with her tweezers. It surprised me how much it hurt and I jerked away even though I was trying hard to be still. She bonked me on the head and said Stop carrying on. Now my eyelids are puffy and red but she says I will thank her later. When, I wonder?

Birthday or not, there isn't much on me that Mother leaves alone. She pokes into my ears to clean them with a swab until sometimes there is blood. She digs the dirt out from under my fingernails and cuts them into pointy shapes. She knuckles me in the back for good posture. My eyes get me into trouble if nothing else does. What are you looking at? she says. Look at me when I am talking to you!

In a dream I had last night she was floating on her back in the swimming tank with no clothes on. Her bosoms were as big as Nanny Wayne's and they were hanging off to the side. Her belly was white and puffy like warm marshmallows. Long hair like the top of corn ears was sticking up between her legs. Her lips and fingernails and toenails were painted smeary bright red. I tried to swim away but she put a power on me and I couldn't move no matter how hard I drove my body from the inside. She said, Come closer! I can show you how to swim the easy way!

So now I am a young lady. I'm not sure what all that will mean but I guess I will find out.

Sunday, July 17, 1960

My hair is the kind that curls all over your head and nothing you can do will stop it. For church Mother french braids it tight onto my scalp to try to get control but even then it creeps out. She says a little bit of curl is good but too much is just tempting the devil.

The only good thing about church besides the hymns is seeing Alva Higgins. Afterwards when I go stand over by the tree with the other kids I feel like I am on one side of a see-through wall they don't know about. If they like me I'm glad, but their liking doesn't quite get to where I am. I want them to be my friends but not because it will make any difference. It's more like charms on a bracelet. It's better to have more.

It only happens with Alva that I don't feel the wall. She talks right into me. She never means anything more than what she says so I don't have to worry about tricks.

I wasn't sure if she liked me or not though, until today when I asked her. Here is what we said:

Me: Do you like me, Alva?

Her: Yes.

Me: I like you, too.

Her: I know.

Me: Are we friends?

Her: Nope. I don't have friends.

Me: Why not?

Her: I just don't. If I did though, you could be one.

Me: I want to be one.

Her: No you don't. You think you do because you don't know.

Me: What do I not know?

Her: What would happen. No one else would play with you. Ladies would tell your mother and she would stop it. Then you would be sadder than if we'd never been friends.

Me: OK, I know you don't have clean clothes and

that's because you don't have a mother or else because she is a Mexican. Either way it's not your fault. I could make people understand that. I know I could.

Her: Look Lou Ann, here's what you need to know. I do have a mother. She does sex with men. Lots of them. Probably your Daddy. Probably everybody's Daddy. She has a place out by the Oklahoma line and she gets the men after they buy the liquor. She takes the money and buys whiskey for herself and my dad. And she is a Mexican. Her name is Juanita. So you can't be my friend.

I couldn't think of what to say next. At least now I know she likes me.

When other kids don't like me I think it's mostly because I don't know how to play for fun. Lots of times things don't seem fair to me and when I say so they get mad and say, It's just a game! Or else I decide to win at something strong like tether ball or arm rassling and I put everything into it, and I sweat and turn red and they say I take things too serious.

But they all want me on the 4th of July when it's time for Red Rover because they know I won't let anyone through even if I fall down from holding on.

When he was walking out of the kitchen after lunch today Lonnie passed me a folded up note. What it said was, I am learning a new song and I would like for you to listen to me sing it. Yours truly, Lonnie.

I threw the note right in the trash and I have already burned it up. I don't think he would've written it if he knew how much trouble he could get me into.

I will try to get out there maybe tomorrow. Today I have to wash the windows so they will look nice when we get curtains. Even though Mother is not mad any more, she is still buying things she says we need. She says she has ordered a surprise for me in my room. It could come any day now.

She has also decided to go to the doctor in Amarillo for her maternity checkup, and she says I can go along. The appointment is for next Monday. She says Dr. Healey in Wheatly has no idea what he's talking about. She wants quality. She's tired of fooling around. She has the name of a doctor that Jewel Wilhite went to when she was having her twins. Jewel says he's good for special cases. When Mother called to make the appointment she told the nurse that she had already lost several babies and wasn't interested in losing this one.

Amarillo is two hours from here, west and a little north. It's the biggest town anywhere near us. Some people go there to shop for school clothes or for a big night out. I've never been, but Mother says not to get excited because this is not a pleasure trip.

Our telephone is on a party line so now it's only a matter of time until Mrs. Barlow at church asks what happened over in Amarillo. Our ring is two longs and a short and no one else is supposed to pick up on that ring, but people do. Whenever Daddy answers the phone he calls out Hello neighbors! before he starts talking to the person who called. Usually the call is about a new tire for the truck or getting more diesel fuel out here, but I guess anything is news to some people.

Tuesday, July 19, 1960

I went out to the bunkhouse before coming here to write. Lonnie sang me a song he made up himself:

At the end of the day when my work is done
And I'm sitting on my bed here all alone
And I'm counting up my blessings one by one
I count you too.

You might be just a friend or you might be more
I can't really tell from what has gone before
But I'm hoping that before you walk out that door
You'll count me too.

Well I've learned to be thankful for what I've got
Even when it seems like it's not a lot
I think you could love me but maybe not
And I need to find out just what is what.

So I'm asking you today, is there any chance
That somebody like me and you could find romance?
Then when they count the pairs up for life's big dance
They'll count us too.

He sang it looking down at his hands while they changed chords. When he finished he looked at me like he was afraid. He said, Well what do you think?

I said I thought it was a beautiful song. I said he sang it as good as the Everly Brothers. I said, Do you write a lot of songs?

Only when I feel something strong, he said.

I asked him to teach me the harmony on it. He had the whole line already thought up and it didn't take me long to learn. He wrote out a pencil copy of the words in case

I forgot. Then we sang it through. We sounded good together, almost like a record.

Then I said I better go. He said Think about them words, Lou Ann.

So I am sitting here doing that. I can't keep my face from smiling. It is a really nice song.

Wednesday, July 20, 1960

I need to write down something that happened so that I won't believe myself when I tell myself it didn't.

In our bathroom we have a high window up next to the ceiling. It is the one place in the house we have always had a curtain. The other night when Mother and I were getting out of the tub I looked up and saw that the curtain was pulled back a little. Someone could do that if they climbed up on the lavatory and reached high. It wouldn't happen by itself. Later I went in and climbed up and fixed it.

The next day after I used the toilet I called Mother to come check my bm. While I was waiting I looked up and saw that the curtain was back open. After Mother gave me Ex-Lax and walked out, I climbed up to fix it and when I did I saw the cherry tree outside shake like somebody had been in it. Then I saw my brother running away toward the tractor he had fueled up. He looked back and saw me seeing him.

After that the curtain stayed put.

I don't like it that my brother was peeking in. But I know if I tell he will get spanked till he drops and he will hate me more than he already does. What I am doing is pretending I didn't see anything. My brother is pretending that too.

Thursday, July 21, 1960

Some days the flies are so slow you can hit them with your hand. Other days they're too fast to hit even with the newest swatter. Before a rain they land on you and bite hard but it doesn't leave a mark after they are gone. I don't know enough about flies to know why any of this is true, but it is. I guess creatures have their ways.

A new Life magazine came today. In it there is a picture of a boy with a whole set of World Book Encyclopedias. They probably tell all about flies. Under the picture it says, "Your child needs help right now to prepare him for the world of tomorrow."

I would like to be prepared for the world of tomorrow. I plan to live there.

I have seen a set of World Books at the library in Wheatly. I like the maps that show where the mountains and forests and deserts are. If I were picking a place to live I could use them to help me decide. They also have maps that show what all is grown in different places and they got it right for here: wheat. Some show how much rain falls every year on average.

One thing I noticed is that all the World Books actually tell about is the past. Maybe that is all there is to help anybody prepare. But I don't see how it will help all that much. If there's no rain next year, how will it help to know how much we got this year? The wheat will still be too dry to grow.

I've also noticed they never put a picture of a girl with the books. Maybe they think we are already prepared. We are not.

It says in Life that a baby is born every seven seconds. I am trying to picture all those babies. It doesn't say if they are born alive or dead like the box children. When Mother has our baby it will be in one of those seconds I guess. I wonder if there is a big clock somewhere that they time them all in on. I would like to see that.

There's a song I have heard where a girl asks her mother, What will I be? I guess she is thinking about the world of tomorrow. I would never ask my mother about that. I'd be afraid of her answer. I will just have to wait and see. In the world of tomorrow there may be things to be that I have never even heard of.

Friday, July 22, 1960

Well well well. This morning when I woke up and went to the bathroom what did I see? Red, that's what, bright on my underwear. I have started ministrating. It didn't hurt at all. I know it means bad things can happen but just for now it's exciting. I feel like I am a painter with one strong color.

I am sure glad Mother told me about it before it happened or I would have been scared to death. Blood is scary on anybody.

She was up fixing breakfast already and I didn't want her stopping for me so I just put in some toilet paper folded up. Then I could have told her while she was washing the dishes and I was drying, but I just kept not doing it. Then after the dishes she went in and layed back down in bed probably because with the baby she is extra tired. I went in and stood by the door to see if she was asleep but I couldn't tell. I whispered out Mother pretty loud but she didn't say anything back. She is wearing the maternity blouse still.

All I needed from her anyway was to show me about the sanitary conveniences. Where they were, how to use them. But I found them myself, in the back of the hall closet up high behind the extra sheets. I used the kitchen stool to climb up. The box is blue and it had all the instructions I needed. Next to the box was a little see-through plastic purse with some elastic that had fasteners and I took that too. I needed it to hold the pad on.

So now I am all fixed up. I am the only one who knows I am doing redness right this minute.

Saturday, July 23, 1960

I am thinking about remembering.

I've heard Daddy say that it doesn't matter what you do to kids before they are four years old because they won't remember it anyway.

It is true that I don't remember much from before then. But I don't think grownups should count on that because some things slip through.

For example I have a memory in my hands of putting

them to the top of my head and feeling something like whiskers there. I know now that it goes with a story I've heard Mother laugh and tell where I was pulling my hair all out when I was one year old. To make me stop they just shaved it off. They were afraid I would pull it out by the roots.

Another memory is more like a picture in my head where Mother is holding her butcher knife to my thumb and asking Are you going to stop sucking it? My brother is crying out loud to make her not cut me. I still have my thumb so I guess she left it on.

Sometimes I come to places inside where it feels like a memory should be but instead there is just a hole, a place that feelings I am having right now can fall into.

I wonder what I will remember from now when I am old. I hope I remember about starting to ministrate and being the only one who knows about it.

I hope I remember the smell that always comes right before rain. I don't know what makes it. It can't be the smell of water because once the rain starts, the smell stops. It can't be dirt or trees getting wet because they don't smell like that after the rain when they are still wet. I think it's the clouds, in the moment when they are so heavy they have to let everything go. When I smell it I get hopeful.

I hope I remember how tornadoes churn and boil pinkish-green, then go black and take whatever they want.

I hope I remember the nights when there are so many stars that I could never count them all even if I started now and kept going until I'm too old to remember. My brother told me that some of them are so far away that by the time their light gets to me, the stars could be dead already. I wouldn't know it until years and years later. I'd be standing out here enjoying dead stars. Will it happen that one night a star I am looking for will be gone because it died way before I was born? Or maybe it's a slower thing, just fading away little by little. I might not even notice.

Sunday, July 24, 1960

Today after church and Sunday dinner Mother hand-washed her maternity blouse and starched and ironed it for the trip to Amarillo tomorrow. We're leaving at 8 in the morning, as soon as we get the breakfast dishes done. We have made sandwiches for the men, six sandwiches apiece to last for dinner and supper. Baloney, cheese, and jelly peanut butter. They can eat them in any order they want. As long as I have been alive we have never had sandwiches two meals in a row, till now.

Mother has told me to bring plenty of things to keep busy with. She gave me five dollars in case I need it. I have to give it back if I don't.

I'm bringing the box children because they need to know what's going on. I told them about her wearing the maternity blouse every day and they do not all agree on what it means. Mike and Jody and Sally think it means that everything is fine and Mother just wants to wear something that really shows that she is having a baby. The rest of them think that if Mother is wearing the same thing every day, even after it gets dirty, something is wrong. It might be something wrong with Mother or something wrong with the baby, or it might be both. That is what they think.

The surprise Mother had ordered for my room was a big poster of three French Poodles. There is a mother and two babies she is looking down at like she loves them but they are a lot of trouble. The babies are looking up like they can't help being so cute. The Poodles are white with aqua bows on their necks and the background is hot pink.

It is not something I would have picked out for myself. But I guess it's nice to have something special on my wall for the first time.

She must have used some more of Nanny Wayne's money to pay for it.

Monday, July 25, 1960

When you are driving along in this kind of country and you see something you don't expect, now that is an amazing day.

We were halfway between Wheatly and Amarillo when the highway stopped being flat. It was enough surprise to be going up and down on hills, but then I saw a huge rock with a flat top. I said Mother! Look!

She said I can't look, I'm driving. But then she looked. She said You never saw a big rock before?

I had to think about that. At Mason Creek there's a rock four people can stand on. I would have said that was a big rock but now I know it wasn't. No ma'am, I said.

Well, that's a mesa. It means table in Spanish, she said. I said How do you know about that? She said Everybody knows about that.

Then we got to the top of another hill and the ground

split open on both sides of the highway, wide and deep, different colors. Brown, gold, green, black, gray.

Palo Duro Canyon, Mother said, before I asked. I know how to spell it now but when she said it, it sounded like Paladura. I asked what that means and she said, How should I know? She said Nice to look at but what a waste of land. Too rocky for farming and not pretty enough for tourists.

The canyon only lasted a few miles. I never took my eyes away. Now I have made myself a promise: I will go back there someday. It isn't wasted on me.

I am writing this in the waiting room at the doctor in Amarillo. This is the first time I have ever written indoors in front of people. No one seems to mind. There's a drug store right next door and I got a nice spiral notebook with some of Mother's money. It's small enough to hide fast. I'll tell her I spent the money on cheese crackers.

The box children are right here next to me. They asked me to keep the covers pulled up over their heads. They remember only bad things from places like this.

This office is much nicer than the one in Wheatly. The furniture is soft couches and there is green carpeting on all of the floor. There's a lady who sits in front just to say hello and make sure the doctor knows you are there. In Wheatly you have to ring a bell for the nurse to come.

The lady told Mother, The doctor will be with you soon, please make yourself at home and just relax. Mother smiled halfway and said Thank you kindly. I have never heard her say that in my life.

She didn't have to wait long and now she is in there, behind a light green door. I tell the box children, Now the doctor is asking her questions. Now he is listening to her heart. Now he is listening for the baby's heart. I don't really know what he is doing but I think it makes them not be so scared. I heard Mike say to Sally, take deep breaths.

The lady in front told me how to spell Palo Duro. She says you can walk down in there. She says cattle get lost at the bottom and the ranchers have to scare them out. She says in a storm, Palo Duro is the place to be. The wind just blows right over.

They have Ladies Home Journals here. The pictures of ladies in them are much fancier than in Life. There's one lady in a beautiful ballgown made to match toilet paper that comes in what they call negligee colors of pale pink, pale green, pale blue, and pale yellow.

There's an advertisement for baby powder that shows a pregnant lady wearing a silky top and pants and earrings and a bracelet. She's halfway lying down on an outdoor couch and there's a wine glass and little cookies on the table. She's playing cards.

I was hoping there would be other kids around, but there's only me and a girl who is older. I asked her if she wanted to play paper dolls and she said No thank you. She was reading a book about frogs. If I want to, I can read Cherry Ames, Student Nurse. I have it right here with me.

My paper doll is named June Allison. She is very beautiful, but also very nice. You can tell. Besides her evening gowns and fur coats, she has dresses to wear to church and everyday clothes just for around the house. She also has a swimsuit and sunglasses and a beach ball. I wonder if she has had any babies. She is skinny so I imagine not. Mother says you gain with every baby and you never really lose it.

I dressed June in a black evening gown with shiny sparkles on the top part and a red rose at the waist. It's for a costume ball, and there is a fancy black mask she is supposed to hold up to cover her eyes. It makes her look like Zorro's bride. I hummed the wedding march and moved June through the air in time to the music. Zorro rode by on his horse and grabbed her up and took her to their hideaway. Then I changed her into a little house dress with a red and white-polka-dotted apron. In her hand was a rolling pin so she could make pies today, apple and cherry. She makes good pies. When they are ready I will eat some, while they're still hot. I'll save some for Zorro. Maybe the girl with the frog book will smell the pie and want some too. We'll put on ice cream and let it melt.

I'm stopping to hide the notebook because I hear Mother coming out now.

Tuesday, July 26, 1960

Yesterday Mother walked out of the doctor's office and right out the door to the parking lot like she forgot I was in the waiting room. The lady in front said Get your stuff honey, I think your mama's all done. I ran out to where the car was parked and she was already zooming the motor up. Take your sweet time, she said. She meant hurry up.

Once we got going I asked her what the doctor said.

She said, Nothing that makes a bit of difference. He said we will just have to wait now for the baby to come out. Now isn't that the smartest thing you've ever heard? What else was I planning on doing the next four months?

I asked if he heard the heartbeat.

He heard whatever there was to hear, she said. My

baby is fine and if there was a problem I'm sure I would know it before any fancy doctor asking all kinds of questions. I'm even thinking of having this one at home since I lost the other ones in hospitals.

Now mind your own business, she said.

She drove us to a bar-be-que place and we had a big meal of salad and ribs and onion rings. She drank a beer before the salad, one with the ribs, and one after while I had tapioca pudding for dessert.

The beers made her sleepy so she got into the back seat of the car and told me to drive us on home. I have driven in the fields but I don't know how to drive on a highway and she knows that. So I just sat in front while she took her nap. A long time went by and I fell asleep too, for a while. The box children woke me up with their crying. They didn't understand what was going on.

Before we left Amarillo we stopped at a store and got more beer. Mother said, Might as well save your Daddy a trip to the line. She got five six packs and put them in the trunk. Don't tell, she said, it's a surprise.

I wanted to go to a sewing shop to get material for the new maternity blouse but she said Not today. By the time we made it home the sky was already orange. I slept for most of the way and missed seeing Palo Duro Canyon again.

I guess everything is OK. I still have 4 dollars left from the money Mother gave me. I'm not giving it back unless she remembers to ask.

Even though I don't take piano lessons in the summer I practice every now and then just to keep in shape. The songs I play are mostly ones Mother and Daddy already like. They tell the piano teacher what music to order, songs they have heard on the radio. Once the teacher snuck me a piece by J. S. Bach to try to figure out but they said We are not paying for lessons just to hear a bunch of notes one after the other. My favorite piece to play is Boogie Mama because of the loud octaves in the left hand. I can really get going on those.

Right after I finished practicing this morning the piano tuner and his wife showed up, Omar and Lanie Hanks. He is blind and she has unusual-shaped legs that pooch way out at the top. Him and her come once every summer, you never know when it will be. She drives the pickup of course.

Omar used to be a farmer. He got blind because he was up trying to fix something on the windmill and his foot slipped off the metal bar and he fell on his head on the sidewalk. Everybody said he was lucky to be alive but he didn't think so. He said any man who had to put his wife to work on a tractor should be shot.

Every time they come, Lanie tells the story while Omar leans into the piano in the corner listening hard to each note and turning the pegs til it sounds right.

She says:

When he first got blind Omar used to cry every single day. I'd wake up in the morning and he'd be crying already. He'd say, I'm no use to anybody any more, I should just kill myself and get it over with. Well, I got so sick of it that finally I just went to the closet, loaded up the shot gun and handed it to him. Then I got in the pickup and drove to town for groceries.

I didn't know if I'd be coming home to a husband or a bloody mess.

When I walked back in the house he was sitting Indian-style in the middle of the kitchen floor smiling like a baby. He said when he held the shotgun up to his head he saw the Lord and the Lord said he should become a piano tuner. So here we are!

When she gets to this part of the story, Lanie spreads both her arms out high like a circus girl after she has just climbed down from the trapeze.

Daddy says he thinks she made up the whole thing so we will pay them more. Mother says she can't imagine making up a story about yourself that has such a big sin in it. If he had done suiside he would have gone straight to hell and Lanie too for helping him do it.

At lunch Daddy said what Omar should have shot off was the top of Lanie's legs. He laughed but Mother didn't. He raised one eyebrow then and said, You better be glad you've got great legs. He pointed a make-believe gun at her. She said, Don't you even pretend to point that thing at me, I've got a baby in here.

While Omar was tuning the piano I noticed that Mother was drinking lots of water from her cup. She even left the room a couple of times to get more. I asked her if I could get it for her and she said no. The funny thing is, I didn't hear the water turn on or the refrigerator door shut. It sounded like she went to the cabinet down below where we keep the groceries. When I looked there later, way in the back I found the beer we got to surprise Daddy. Quite a bit of it is gone already.

I guess she is drinking it hot. Daddy only likes it cold.

My brother came out to the barn just as I was climbing down from playing in the wheat bin yesterday. He said, Brick Farrell says you french kissed him on the 4th of July.

I told him I did not. I told him Brick Farrell snuck up on me and swirled his tongue all over my mouth but I didn't do anything back. My brother said That's not the way Brick tells it. He says you might have gone all the way if he hadn't stopped you.

He's a big liar! I said.

Mother can be the judge of that, he said. I'm telling her unless you show me what you did with Brick. I said, What do you mean show you?

He said, Just show me how you did it. Then I won't tell.

That would be like kissing you, I said.

No it wouldn't, it would just be showing me what you did with Brick, he said. I said I would show him on the back of his hand.

He said, No, that's gross.

Well that's all I will do, I said, Do you want it or not?

He said What if I tell Mother I've seen you out in the bunkhouse with Lonnie Helfenbein? Lonnie will get fired and it will be all your fault.

For a minute I couldn't think of what to say to that.

Then I said, I'll tell her you were peeking in the bathroom window.

What if I tell her you've been writing a diary? he said.

How do you know that? I said.

I know everything about you, he said. Show me or I'll give it to Mother.

He moved over close and bent his mouth down to mine.

There was nothing else to do. I held my breath and swirled my tongue on his lips. Then fast he opened his mouth and started licking my tongue with his. He was grabbing onto me and I couldn't get away so I bit down hard. I made his mouth bleed. He tried to slap me but I was gone.

I ran straight out to the barrel where I keep the diary and looked under. Nothing was there. I got sick to my stomach right on the spot. When I went back to the barn, my brother was nowhere.

If I had not bit him he might have given it back right then. Instead I got mad and forgot what was most important. Now I would do just about anything to get it back.

At dinner my brother would not look at me. He couldn't eat much because of his hurt mouth. Now we both have something we are afraid the other one will tell Mother.

I am putting this page between my two mattresses in the center of the bed. I don't know where else to put it. Nothing is really safe now.

Things get worse and worse. When I sent my big letter to Wyn Rue I accidentally put the wrong house number on it. No one named Wyn lives where I sent it so it came back here. While I was outside yesterday Mother opened it up and read everything.

She rang the bell for me and when I got to the porch she said Lou Ann, is there anything you want to tell me? I was so scared my brother had given her the diary that I couldn't even say a word. Then she marched me to the kitchen table to see the display she had made. At one end of the table was Wyn's letter and at the other end were six sanitary conveniences lined up in a neat row. That's all that was left after I took what I needed for my four days of redness. I guess she counted them up.

So now Mother knows I went outside at night and kissed a Wheatie. She knows Brick put his tongue on my mouth. She knows I lied to her twice in the forms of sending a letter she had not read first and not telling her about my first ministration. She says that is the worst thing, that I became a woman without even telling her.

But for me the worst thing was that I told Wyn Rue I had a diary. Mother hit and hit to get me to show it to her but I told her it was a big lie. I told her I only said I had a diary to impress Wyn because I was jealous that she had one. Finally I said How could I have a diary without you knowing it? That made her believe me. If she had hit me all the way dead I would never have told her the truth.

She said the lie about the diary was just more proof that I am evil and deseatful. She says unless she can cure me, I am on my way straight to the devil. Spanking me with the wooden paddle my brother made was the first part of the cure. She started with ten licks and she will add one every day until she feels like it's working.

She has decided to make the punishment fit the crime. She says if I am going to act like a cheap tramp then she is going to have to start treating me like one. She says since I think I'm a such a grownup woman now I have to wear rouge and lipstick all the time and high heel shoes. And she made me a tramp dress out of some old red shiny material. She also gave me one of her big bras and had me stuff wads of toilet paper into it. She said every tramp needs a good set of falsies.

She took down the poodle poster in my room and put up a girlie calendar from the bunkhouse. Every hour or so she freshens up my lipstick and rouge.

She said there will be no more letters. She says if I'm not going to tell her everything that happens to me, then she will just not let me out of her sight. Today she even came with me into the bathroom. From the very minute I woke up this morning she was right there. If she was busy doing something, I had to just stay in the room with her. I sat quiet in her room while she took her nap.

The thing is, at night she has to sleep with Daddy. She's in there sleeping right now. I am writing under my own covers.

I like the red dress material and I don't really mind the lipstick. It looks nice and since I started ministrating I would have had to start wearing it soon anyway. The spankings hurt but I am kind of used to that.

But all of this is silly compared to not knowing where my writing is. There's no way to find out about it with Mother being right there all the time.

It could be that my only writing is what I will do from now on.

Saturday, July 30, 1960

Mother made me wear the whole tramp outfit all day yesterday. She told me that she'd expect me to serve supper while she sat down to rest her feet. While I was setting the table I checked her cup and beer was in there again.

When the men came in to eat she said, I want you all to enjoy Lou Ann today. She thinks she is a red hot tomato. She wants to be the kind of lady a man might like to mess with out in the barn. I want you to show her what she has to look forward to. Come on now, don't be shy. Give her a little pinch on the bottom, or you could slip a dollar or two in that nice big bosom of hers.

Nobody said anything. Mother looked over at Buck Davis and said, Lou Ann, I think Buck needs some more iced tea, would you please pour him some? When I did, she said, Sit on down there on his lap and show him a good time why don't you? You'd like that, wouldn't you Buck?

Buck just sat there. Mother got up and pushed me hard onto his lap and then put his hand up on the falsie. There, she said. Isn't that nice? My daughter is really making a place for herself in the world.

Buck took his hand away and tried to get me off of him but Mother pushed me back on. She said Mr. Davis, as long as you work on my farm you will do what I say. Tuck a little money down in between those pretty bosoms, would you please now?

Buck said, I don't have any money, ma'am.

Well now that is just the problem with you boys, you never have any money do you? Mother said. Remember that, Lou Ann, she said. And get down off of there, I wouldn't want you to get all comfortable.

I kept thinking Daddy would say something to stop her but he just sat there looking worried. My brother looked scared to me. He probably thinks I told Mother about the kiss.

The rest of the meal Mother didn't make me sit on anybody else. She just said things like Lou Ann you are going to have to wiggle that bottom of yours a lot more if you want to catch a man. Or It's better if you bend over more in the man's face so they can get a good look at what you've got to offer.

I just did whatever she said. I think if I can be a good tramp for a few days she'll get tired of the whole thing. By that time maybe I will have my diary back and everything will be different.

I'm glad she didn't make me sit on Lonnie.

Sunday, July 31, 1960

Mother let me wear normal clothes to church. But then when we were leaving she went up to Alva Higgins and said, I think it's time you came out for a visit.

Alva could tell I wanted her to come so she did.

When we got to the house Mother sent me in to put on the tramp outfit. I didn't have a chance to tell Alva what all is going on. She just kept her eyes on everything and pretty much figured it out.

At the dinner table Mother said, Gentlemen, I want to introduce to you Miss Alva Higgins, a friend of my daughter's. You all probably are familiar with Miss Higgins' mother I am sure. I am hoping that Alva can tell us a little about what her mama does for a living and what a nice home she has made for her family.

Alva looked straight at Mother and said, I don't have a mama.

Well now we all know that's not true, Mother said. Telling a lie is only adding to the problems you already have, don't you think?

Alva said, There's a lady who had me but she is not my mama. Nobody is. I make my own home.

And I can tell by your lovely dress and hair-do that you are doing a truly wonderful job, Mother said. Lou Ann, trampy ladies have daughters who look like Alva and even those daughters are ashamed of them. Is that what you think you want?

I was too mad to even talk. Alva stood up from the table and said, I think I will be walking home now. I got up to go with her but Mother knocked me back down.

She said, It's bad manners to leave before the hostess has even finished serving the meal.

Alva was already out the door.

Then Mother said, I hope you see what kind of a girl your little friend is, Lou Ann. She won't have any trouble getting someone to pick her up along the road. Maybe one of you gentlemen here would like to go out and give her a little ride?

Nobody said a word.

I don't so much mind if Mother has to be mean to me but the way she was to Alva made me sick. My stomach hurt bad all afternoon but I didn't want to have to take Castor Oil so I just kept quiet. I hope Alva got home OK and that she'll be able to forgive me. I should have known to tell her not to come.

One thing Mother doesn't know is that at church I gave Alva a letter with the right address to mail to Wyn Rue, and money for the stamp. I told Wyn to write me back at Alva's house and Alva will give me the letter.

There are ways to get things done.

Lonnie has my diary!

He put a note under his plate for me to find when I cleared the table. He takes chances even I would never take. I had to keep the note in my hand until Mother turned away for just a second and I put it under my falsie. Now it's night and I have read it here in bed.

It says: Dear Lou Ann, I have your diary papers. Your brother was showing them off (don't worry no one looked) so I stole them when he was asleep. He thinks you did it. I have put them in my lock box so they are safe. You can have them back whenever you want and I promise I won't read them. I know how I would feel if someone got hold of my songs. Also I think you might not know that your mama is crazy. I don't know what is wrong with her but she is not even close to what I would call regular. I have had words with Les and Buck about this and they said to stay out of other folkses problems and if you tell me to that is what I will do. But I can't hardly stand it. At least I can tell you that. Yours truly, Lonnie. P.S. Put a note under my plate when you set the table tomorrow.

I have answered him already. My note says: Dear Lonnie, Thank you thank you thank you for getting me back my diary. I will never be able to pay you back for how much that matters to me. Maybe you could just keep it in your box for now until I can figure out a safe place. I'm sorry you feel so bad about Mother and me. I think it will be over pretty soon. I get mad too but that is just how it is. Sometimes she is nice. Anyway thank you again really much for the diary. Yours truly, Lou Ann.

I know Mother is mean sometimes but I don't think she's crazy. Crazy people live in insanasilums.

We are up to 13 spank hits. She does it after the bath when my clothes are already off.

My writing is found! Nothing my brother can do will hurt me now.

Tuesday, August 2, 1960

You never know when things will get worse again.

Daddy left early this morning. He said he had to go to Elk City, Oklahoma for some parts. After lunch Mother said let's go for a little drive. I had on my tramp outfit and she had on her maternity blouse like always.

We headed straight for the state line. When I asked where we were going Mother said she needed some special ingredients for a sauce she was making. At the liquor store she told me to wait in the car. I have done that with Daddy but never with Mother. I looked all around and what I saw was a white shack off the highway one hundred yards or so. A pickup like Daddy's was parked behind it.

After a while, a man came out of the liquor store with a couple of flat boxes and Mother opened the trunk for him to put them there. The man said We don't get that many ladies out this way, ma'am, especially not ones in a family way. That's a nice looking daughter you got there in the car.

You are exactly the type of man who would think so, Mother said.

I looked in the other direction from the shack when she got in the car, but it didn't keep her eyes from going over there. She saw the pickup and it made her take in her breath so fast she started coughing hard. I said Are you OK but she just kept coughing. Then she went and opened the trunk and took out two beers and drank them hot one after the other. We sat there in the car while she drank and coughed and stared across the road.

Finally she said, I have a better idea now about the new parts your Daddy had in mind to get. She drove over in front of the shack and started honking the car horn in a rhythm like jazzy music. Then she started singing La Cucaracha with made up Mexican words for most of it.

Between honking and singing she said Run on up to that door, Lou Ann, and tell Juanita Higgins you're a friend of her daughter's. Tell her you're here to take some hore lessons because your Daddy likes hores so much.

I didn't move a muscle. I was remembering that Alva did say her mama's name was Juanita.

After a while a Mexican lady came out on the porch with a shotgun. She had the same straight look on her face as Alva has, and she was kind of pretty. She said This is my property and I would politely like you to get the hell off of it.

Mother said YOUR property! You got MY property in there! Why don't you just shoot HIM with that shotgun of yours and then I'll leave you BOTH alone!

Daddy must have gone out some back door because the next thing I saw was him driving his pickup around onto the highway. Mother took out after him. The rocks in the driveway made us spin around before we got straight and headed down the road home. I've never gone that fast with Mother. It was more like the times in the pickup when Daddy takes me out in the field to shoot jackrabbits. He steers with one hand and shoots the shotgun with the other. The loose dirt in the field keeps us slipping all around. The jackrabbits go in all directions and Daddy jerks the wheel back and forth to stay up on them. Some get away and some do not.

Driving the car Mother did look crazy. I wanted to get out but I think that might have killed me. I kept imagining myself opening the door and jumping. If I had, I don't think she would have stopped to see if I was OK. Daddy is all she was thinking on.

Pretty soon instead of racing to catch up she just let him get way on ahead. She started talking to herself. She kept saying, If Bill Campbell wants hores, I'll give him hores.

At dinner she acted like nothing at all happened so I know she is planning something. Daddy was too scared to say a word.

Wednesday, August 3, 1960

Right after breakfast Mother went to town without me. She took some beers with her. She came back with things from the drug store to make her hair blond and now it is. She had me curl it and comb it out poofy. She also got some more calendars with naked ladies and put them up around the kitchen. She said, We want your Daddy to feel right at home.

She rang the dinner bell at noon and told me to go ahead and start serving the macaroni and cheese. She went back into the bedroom and shut the door. She came in a few minutes later in a pink see-through house robe with nothing on under it. You could see everything. She had on high heels and was smiling like Miss America.

Lonnie got right up from the table and walked out the door. Les and Buck and my brother stared with their mouths open and then looked down at their plates. Daddy jumped up and grabbed a tea towel from the sink to cover her up with but when he tried, she picked a butcher knife up off the cabinet and said Don't you touch me.

Then she went back to smiling. She said, Tell your friends I am open for business.

She walked around the kitchen looking at the calendars and then sat down on the floor in one of the poses, where the lady puts her hands behind her head with her elbows sticking out. The feet are folded over to the side and the bosoms point up. Mother's hung down but otherwise it looked the same.

She said, Come over here Lou Ann, you're always wanting to make your Daddy happy. Pick one of these ladies to style yourself on.

The thing is, I had already looked at the calendar she put in my room and I knew the pose I liked. It's where she stands with her back facing the camera and her elbows up and out. She turns her neck all the way around so you can see her face smiling. But I didn't want to do it in front of anybody.

So I was glad when Daddy said That's enough Loretta. He grabbed the knife away and threw it in the sink. He tried to pick her up but the robe was slippery and he didn't know where to grab with her naked underneath.

How would you know what's enough? she said. A baby on the way and you can't keep your hands off hores.

A baby on the way, Daddy said. And where is that baby, Loretta? With what you've got on everyone can see where it ought to be but you're no fatter than ever. After five months of cooking, the bread should be rising a little more by now.

I made myself look at her there. In the bathtub I never look, but with the maternity blouse on it seemed like she was showing good. She is not.

I'm carrying small, she said. She looked sad there on the floor. I could tell she was ready to be done with the see-through robe so I got her the tea towel. She covered her front with it while she stood up and then backed over to the door.

She raised up her arm straight and pointed at Daddy with her finger stiff. She was shaking all over. I want you out, she said. You're a bad influence on the children. Les and Buck can take care of everything here including me. The last thing I need on my farm is a man who can't say no to the devil. It's only a matter of time till you run everything to ruin.

Come on now Loretta, Daddy said. You know I love this farm and I love you. I'm one of the best farmers there is, even your daddy says so.

If my daddy had seen what I saw yesterday you would be a dead man, she said. I want you out by the time the sun goes down and I don't want you to ever come back. My heart is broken but at least I can make a Christian home for my children.

So that was that. Daddy got some things together and left in the pickup. Mother got some beers and shut the door to the bedroom and hasn't come out since. I changed out of the tramp outfit and I'm not wearing it again. I don't think it really belongs in a Christian home.

I made sandwiches for supper. The men were all talking about what needs to be done tomorrow. With Daddy gone, Les seems to be the boss. He likes it, you can tell. He told everybody what jobs he wants them to do. He said it's a safe bet that Daddy will be back but til then we have to make sure things stay in good shape.

Buck, he said, I'm putting you in charge of Loretta. Buck hooted. Les said Do whatever she wants. She's the real boss here.

After the men left and I had cleared the table Lonnie knocked on the back door and asked if I needed some help with the dishes. I will write about that tomorrow. Sometimes too much happens for one day.

When I said goodnight to the box children I decided not to tell them about Mother not showing because they were so happy to see me in regular clothes. They didn't like looking at me trampy.

Thursday, August 4, 1960

This morning Mother was all cheerful. She had on the maternity blouse and she didn't say anything about what I was wearing. I think she looks good with the blond hair.

Before breakfast she took down all the calendars including the one in my room and in their place she has put up pictures of Jesus. Not just his face but more like in scenes from different Bible stories. One has him with little children all around like he's telling a good story. In one he's riding a donkey in a parade. Another shows him giving out food at a picnic.

She wanted to know if I thought the men would like having pancakes. That is usually a special Saturday morning breakfast. I said sure they'd like it but it might make them sleepy on the tractors. She said They can stop and take naps. No harm in it.

She makes great pancakes, thick and fluffy. She cooks them on an electric griddle 6 at a time and we eat each batch as it comes off hot. We warm up the Karo and we have both kinds, light and dark. Daddy likes molasses but everyone else thinks it's nasty. With him gone I didn't even have to put it on the table.

Buck asked Mother if she had anything special she needed done today. She said thank you but that if she did, she would ask my brother to do it. She said Family takes care of family.

My brother said, When is Daddy coming back?

Mother acted like she didn't hear the question. Les said I guess things happen when they happen.

I have been so mad at my brother but today without Daddy around he seems different. Looking at him makes me sad.

When I let Lonnie in the door last night he said Do you want me to bring the diary papers to you?

I said No I think they are safer in your lockbox, can I give you more to put there? He said Yes, and I went and got them. Then he said Do you believe me now?

I said About what? He said, Your mama being crazy.

I do know what he means. There are some things she does that are like some story you would hear about some person who could be about to lose their mind.

But I didn't like Lonnie just saying it straight out like that. Even if she is crazy there is not a thing I can do about it. And anyway it isn't all the time.

I said What about your own mama? How come she makes you live with some other family and work as hard as a grown man?

He said My mama has nine kids with no daddy because he died. She is crazy in a sad way, not mean like your mama. She has a real hard time getting anything done. I seen her spend a whole day at the window just looking out.

I can picture that.

Lonnie said he wouldn't care how my mama is except for me. He says he's lucky to be out of his house for the summer and I should get out of this one too. I told him HE is crazy. For now at least, this is where I live.

He dried the dishes while I washed. I told him men aren't supposed to do dishes and he said There's no law about it.

Friday, August 5, 1960

I have the box children with me because we need to talk about Mother.

I told them It's time for her to be growing but instead she is staying her same size. She's acting like nothing is wrong but that can't be true. This baby is not going to make it.

The children wouldn't give up.

Mike: Maybe she just hasn't been eating enough.

Jim: Make her ice cream sodas every day and see if she grows.

Jody: Make her a new maternity blouse, the baby

won't grow in that one because the pattern is too scary.

Molly: Some ladies just carry little.

Sally: She's probably just holding her tummy in so she won't look fat.

I had to tell them to stop making up ways the baby will be OK because it will not. The time for hoping is over. They started crying and they kept on a long time. I cried with them. I pictured myself holding the baby in the rocking chair, singing a song real quiet. It was a sweet baby. Its eyes looked right in mine. There was nothing we didn't know together.

The children asked Why would Mother act like the baby is fine if it isn't? I said I think she wants this baby so bad she is a little crazy. After I said that I started wondering if there even was a real baby in there. If she is crazy she might have made it all up in the first place.

I didn't say that to the box children. In our hearts we have made a place for this baby and losing it hurts the same whether or not it's real.

I told the box children that I love them no matter what. They love me too. I'm all they have.

No news about Daddy.

I was hoping Mother would make pancakes again this morning but when I woke up she was still in bed. It was only a few minutes until the men would be in for a breakfast we hadn't even started on yet.

I knocked on her door and she said Go away. Then she said What do you want? She sounded real sleepy. I said, Time to make breakfast. She said Shit. I decided to open the door. That is not a word my mother says.

Beer cans were all over the floor. Mother had on her maternity blouse all wrinkled from being slept in.

Get me some water, she said. So I did. When I came back she was sitting with her legs hanging over the bed. She said Get me out some clean underwear. While she got herself into them I put my eyes on a picture of Jesus standing at a wishing well.

Get on in the kitchen, she said. Make toast. Crack a bowl of eggs for me to scramble. Everything is fine.

We got breakfast on the table fast. We didn't have meat because there wasn't time to cook it. If Daddy was here he'd have said something about that but no one else did. I think my brother and the men were just glad to have anything at all on their plates. Mother was moving slow like everything hurt.

She told Les and Buck and Lonnie to take the weekend off. She gave them money so they could eat hamburgers in town at the Sunrise Cafe. I would like to do that with them. But that will not happen.

Les said, Can we get you anything from town, Loretta? She said, A new husband. Nobody laughed. My brother said, Isn't Daddy coming back?

Not unless you stop asking about him, Mother said. She only said that to shut him up. The truth is my brother has nothing to do with it. It's all up to Mother.

Her plan for my brother and me today was to ride around in the car with her all afternoon. She didn't say what we were doing but we were looking for Daddy. We all knew that. We didn't see his pickup anywhere. I don't know what she would have done if she had found him. I guess it would depend on where he was and what he was doing at the time.

I dreamed last night that I was not born yet. I was still inside Mother and it was time to come out. I had a choice: Go out, or give up. Things had already been hard and I knew they wouldn't get better for a long time if I picked "out." But if I gave up I'd never know the rest of the story. I wanted to know.

The box children must have decided it wasn't worth it. I am the one putting them in the story after they already took themselves out.

Sunday, August 7, 1960

I was halfway expecting Daddy to just come to church and sit with us like nothing had happened. I guess he probably doesn't have his suit and tie with him. Everyone noticed he was not there. When they asked about him Mother said he wasn't feeling good. Which is probably true.

The other thing they noticed was Mother's blond hair. She wore a hat but still you could tell. When people said compliments Mother held her back real straight and her mouth tight in a smile to say thank you. Some of the compliments were not that nice. I think blond might not be as comfortable as your own hair color for church.

Afterwards I saw Alva for the first time since she was at our house for lunch. I told her how sorry I am and she said Stop it, you didn't do anything. Then she said I should know that everybody knows Daddy got turned out and they all know why. She said it is just about all anyone is talking about.

I said, How come they are acting to Mother like they don't know? She said So they can laugh later.

Alva said Daddy is living out of his pickup and doing odd jobs over in Ginnett to earn some money. She has heard some people say All he would have to do is ask for help. The people who are saying that are the last people on earth you would ever want to ask for anything.

In the afternoon Doneva Boone and her daughter Ramona came out to visit. I was surprised because they aren't that good of friends. Ramona is two years older than me and has green eyes like Daddy's. Her daddy has been dead since before she was born. I thought maybe she would want to swim. We have extra suits in lots of sizes.

But it turned out that all Ramona and I got a chance to do was stand around in the kitchen and listen while Mrs. Boone got right to business. She said The reason I came, Loretta, is to let you know I saw your husband over in Wheatly yesterday. He was at the appliance store looking at refrigerators. I couldn't help but notice he had on dirty old clothes and he needed a shave real bad. I spoke up friendly because that's the kind of person I am. I said Bill Campbell, I'm surprised Loretta would let you out of the house looking like that.

Mother said, He was looking at refrigerators?

Deluxe models, Mrs. Boone said. Anyway he said to me, I'm hoping she'll let me back IN the house looking like this. Mrs. Boone stopped and waited to see if Mother was going to explain anything. Mother was not.

I don't have to tell you, Loretta, that lots of women would have asked Bill Campbell to come on over and get cleaned up at their house, Mrs. Boone said.

What color refrigerators? Mother said.

They have any color you want, Mrs. Boone said. Bill was looking at blue. He asked me what I thought you would like. I said Only the best for Loretta. But you are missing my point here, Mrs. Boone said. My point is that I left Bill Campbell at that appliance store looking like he needed a shower and a good meal. If I see him again I will make sure he gets what he needs. I'm just telling you fair and square.

Mother said, If you see him again you tell him I want the RCA Whirlpool Refrigerator-Freezer with the glide-out shelves and the instant ice ejector. Aquamarine is the color. Now get out of my house before I throw you out too.

Mrs. Boone took her time walking out. When she went by our old refrigerator she said, Maybe Bill has his own ideas about the features he wants in a new model.

Monday, August 8, 1960

Lonnie says Daddy has to come back before planting. Les and Buck don't know how to do it by themselves. Lonnie will have to leave pretty soon to start school. He still has two more years to go, over in Wammuck where his mama lives. He said he wants to work for us again next summer, if Daddy comes back. He said I am part of the reason he wants to be here.

I knew that.

Mother has me sleeping with her now. She doesn't like to sleep by herself. She moved my brother in from the bunkhouse to the back porch bed. She says there has to be a man in the house. In bed she reaches her arm under my arm and pulls my back into her front. She says that is the way she cuddles with Daddy. She breathes in and out on my neck hot. I can hardly stand it.

I need Daddy to come home soon.

Tuesday, August 9, 1960

Sometimes I imagine what I would do in bad situations. Like if I fell down on the highway and there was a big truck coming. I would line myself up right between the tires and hold my breath. In a few seconds it would be over and I would check to see if I was alive or not.

Or if I was on a narrow road in the high Rocky Mountains and the car door came open and I fell out and went over the cliff. I would grab hold of a tree branch that would be growing out of the rocks and hold on till someone came to help. If that branch broke I would grab the next one down. I could do that all the way to the bottom if I had to.

But when I try to picture what I would do if I fell out of a boat in the ocean, I can't make it come out good. I always drown. Even if I send along something for myself to hang onto, I can never quite reach where that is. I feel myself getting so scared I forget to breathe and then I just give up the picture because it isn't fun any more. The water closes over where my head was.

Last night I needed to go to the bathroom and I dreamed I got up to go. In the dream, there was no moon out the window and it was so dark that I couldn't see my own hands or feet when I got out of bed. I felt my way into the hallway and somehow got all turned around so that I didn't know where I was any more. I bumped into a wall that had paint sticking up in sharp bumps. I ran into a heater. I turned around and around trying to figure out where I was. I started crying with no noise. I thought that from now on I would always be lost and it would always be dark. I thought I had gone too far. Then in the dream Alva was there in her nightgown saying What's the matter? I said I'm trying to get to the bathroom but I'm lost. She took me by the shoulders and guided me down the hall, just a little farther than I had gone yet, and there was the bathroom.

In real life I almost wet Mother's bed because I thought I was already sitting on the toilet. I woke up just in time.

Wednesday, August 10, 1960

Yesterday Mother kept running to look out the front window. She said she thought she heard somebody coming down the road. The mail man came, and two pickups went by on their way somewhere else.

Now today she is making curtains and putting them up. She's using black material too thick to see through. So far she has done the kitchen and living room but she plans on doing the whole house. When she's done no sun will come in at all.

The curtains made it dark when the men came in for lunch. We're used to dark meals at night but not at noon.

Les said, Hey Loretta, are you trying to create a romance mood here? Mother said That is the last thing on earth I am trying to do.

Then she made a speech. Windows are the devil's way of causing me trouble, she said. First I look out and I see things I wish I had not seen. Then I look out hoping to see things that aren't there. I believe the Christian way is to stop looking out at all. Just be happy with whatever God puts right in front of me. These curtains are a gift from Jesus to help me be happy. Now shut up and eat your food.

When lunch was over she said Lou Ann, I'm too tired to move. You can take care of the dishes can't you. It was not a question. She took her beer and closed the door to the bedroom.

I was wishing Lonnie could help me with the dishes again but he had to get back out to the field. It was so dark in the kitchen I couldn't tell if I got the plates clean or not. I couldn't even see the flowers that are painted on them.

Mother must have forgotten about God saying Let there be light.

Thursday, August 11, 1960

I stayed outside today as much as I could because of the curtains, so I saw him first. Before I could even tell the color of the pickup I knew it was him, just from the way the dust was flying off the road. I ran out to the mailbox to wait.

When he got there he hopped out of the pickup and hollered Hey Lou Ann, how's my girl? He scooped me up high above his head. His whiskers were all shaved and he had a nice haircut. For the first time I was glad about the curtains because Mother wouldn't forgive me if she'd seen him say hello to me first.

In the back of the pickup was a man in brown overalls sitting next to a tall brown box. Run get your mother, Daddy said. I said She might be taking a nap and she gets mad if I wake her up. He said Tell her Bill's here with her Whirlpool.

So I went in and said it just like that, Bill's here with your Whirlpool. It took her a minute to know what I meant. Then she ran over to the living room window and pushed the curtain away so she could see out. Well I'll swan, she said. That's what Nanny Wayne says when she is really surprised.

Mother said, Tell him he should come knock on the front door like company.

That made him laugh. He headed straight for the front door and stood there with one hand holding his hat and the other knocking. It's a solid oak door Daddy Wayne made so it doesn't make much sound, but Mother heard it. Coming! she said like a song.

He said, Delivery here for you, ma'am.

She said, I don't remember ordering a thing.

He said, The way I heard tell, it's from a man who figures he has one chance to prove how sorry he is. He is hoping an RCA Whirlpool Refrigerator-Freezer in aquamarine will do it.

Well, she said, I suppose you could bring it on in here and let me take a look. I could decide then if I want to keep it or send it back.

He pulled the pickup around to the back porch steps and got the man in the brown overalls to help him waggle the refrigerator onto the porch and into the kitchen. He asked Mother for a knife to cut the box away and she gave him her biggest one. When he was done he stood there next to the new refrigerator, side by side with the old one.

There is no one on earth who would not have picked the new one. Daddy said, I can leave it here for a few days for you to try out and you can send it back if you decide you don't want it.

Oh no, Mother said, I'll be keeping it.

She opened it up and noted all the features out loud. Glide out trays, twin crispers, butter conditioner, egg compartment, door shelves, air purifier, she said. Automatic defrost. And ice water tap! Bill, you got me an ice water tap!

I knew you wanted all the conveniences, he said.

Plug it in, she said. Daddy had to move the old one out of the way first, and before he could do that I had to empty out all the cold food onto the table. After he plugged it in, she started arranging it all into the new refrigerator shelves with the tall stuff in back and all the labels facing frontwards.

Then she pointed to the old refrigerator and said, Get that thing out of my house. Take it out back and later on you can see if some poor people want it.

She watched Daddy and his helper move it out there. Then I saw her turn and look at herself in the back porch mirror. Her blond hair was all oily and she had on the dirty wrinkled maternity blouse, but she smiled into the mirror like she was one of the ladies from the magazines.

Friday, August 12, 1960

So Daddy is back. He and Mother are acting like a movie star couple. Daddy kind of looks like a movie star but Mother still hasn't washed her hair. She says it will just get dirty again. It's starting to look unusual. I asked her if she wanted me to help her with it and she said, They spend all that time drilling for oil and here I am producing my own! She laughed and laughed. I guess it is a good joke.

I'm glad to be back to my own bed at night. My brother asked if he could stay sleeping on the back porch and Daddy said OK. It's almost fall anyway and once school starts my brother comes in. The bunkhouse is freezing in the winter.

Also my brother has started to look at my eyes with his every now and then. I don't know about him but now that my diary is safe I am ready to forget about anything else that happened.

Daddy has the hired hands painting the kitchen aquamarine with light gray trim for the cabinets, the way Mother wants. With three people working it will be done in one day. Mother says the paint fumes are bad for the baby so she is staying in the bedroom. Buck said If Loretta has a baby in there then pigs can drive tractors.

Lonnie said Just be glad she's not in here telling us how to paint. That got the biggest laugh of all.

I took some chicken out to thaw and Daddy is planning to bar-be-que it outside for supper. We'll eat on the back porch steps so no one will take chances on messing up the new paint. By tomorrow it will be dry.

Daddy asked me if I could help get Mother's hair back to its real color. I'm surprised at that. I thought he would like it blond. I told him I can wash it if she lets me but I have no idea how to make it brown again. We would have to go to Boolie's Beauty Bar in Wheatly to find that out. Boolie is a real person and I would not mind asking her, but Daddy said he would rather keep it to ourselves.

Now I'm thinking of brown things I could put in her hair that might work. Wooster sauce? Molasses? Motor oil? Chocolate syrup? Maybe if you mix them.

Saturday, August 13, 1960

I was looking forward to going into town for ice cream cones this afternoon with Mother but it looks like that will not happen. She has cut off all her hair.

Daddy was helping her fix breakfast this morning because she had a headache. He was fixing his special scrambled eggs where he leaves sausage bits in the pan with the grease and every bite of the eggs has good flavor in it. She was resting at the table while I set it.

Daddy said, I think today would be a good day for Lou Ann to help you with your hair, Loretta. Maybe when you go to town you can get some brown coloring at the drug store and then Lou Ann can wash it in for you.

She said, I thought you would like it this way. I guess I don't know what you like any more. Maybe you don't even like me. Then she started to cry.

He said I like your hair that way it really is. Isn't that better than if I wanted you all different?

She said, If you like the real me so much why were you always poking your sugar stick around all over the county? While you were gone every woman in town was hoping you might stop by for a quick visit. You think I never knew? Now you're standing there telling me how to fix my own hair. You and trampy old Lou Ann are gonna fix me right up, yes siree. You can both go straight to hell which you probably will do anyway with no help from me.

I had just put a flowery plate and water glass in front of her and she wiped them off the table in a swoop. Oops, she said. One more mess for Lou Ann to clean up. She stepped over the broken glass and headed off to the bedroom.

She'll feel better a little later on, Daddy said. He stood

there stirring his eggs like everything was fine. I picked up the big pieces of plate first and then got the broom and dustpan for the slivers.

How come you don't like her hair blond? I said.

It looks cheap, he said. You don't want your wife looking like that.

I said Mavie Garner's hair looks pretty nice blond don't you think?

He said Mavie Garner is exactly how you don't want your wife to be.

But you like her, I said.

Where did you get that? he said.

From you kissing her in the barn, I said. That's what started all this trouble. And her hair is blond. So you should let Mother have blond hair if she wants to.

Daddy put the eggs on a plate and brought them over to the table were I was. He put his hand on my shoulder and his voice was real low. He said, You pay too much attention to things, honey. Sometimes things just happen and they don't mean anything. The lesson to learn here is to mind your own business and forget when bad things happen. Otherwise you just make trouble. Understand? He rubbed his hand on my back slow and I got the shivers.

We heard Mother's door open and then there she was standing in the kitchen doorway with her cut off blond hair in one hand and her good sewing scissors in the other. The hair on her head looked like the wheat stubble after harvest.

Sunday, August 14, 1960

There isn't really anything you can say to someone who has chopped their hair off. If you say It looks nice, they know you're lying. It doesn't help to say It will grow back soon. It can't possibly be soon enough. I think the best you can do is not be afraid to look right at them and take them serious. After all it's only hair.

Once one of my paper dolls needed her hair cut but she was afraid because she had never had it done before. I cut my hair in front to show her it didn't hurt. Mother spanked me for ruining my hair but I didn't care about that. What hurt was the way Mother looked at me every day while it grew in, like I was not who she wanted any more.

Now Mother will not come out of the bedroom. What happened is that when my brother and I figured out we wouldn't be going to church, we set up chairs in a row in the living room to make up for it. It's the first nice thing we have done together in a long time. We invited Daddy and the hired hands to come in for a home service. I played the two hymns I know real well, Work for the Night is Coming and Holy Holy Holy, and everybody sang. We thought it would help Mother to hear the church music. The room was all dark from the curtains but according to the preacher the holy spirit can go anywhere if you invite it.

My brother did the sermon. He spoke on God Loves Families. He said poor God doesn't have a wife and His son was killed by earthlings so He needs us all to stick together to cheer Him up. Even though the son came back to live forever in heaven it wasn't the same, my brother said. God never got over what the people on earth did.

I never heard a real preacher say that but it did make sense. Then I remembered one more hymn I know, Bringing in the Sheaves, so we sang that. Sheaves was another word for wheat stalks I think, before they had combines that chop them all up.

When we were done my brother knocked on the bedroom door and Mother said Don't come in. You could tell she was crying a lot. My brother just opened the door anyway which I would not have done but since he did it I went in too.

Mother's face was too messed up for words. She had a scarf tight around her head. Beer cans were all around. My brother said Are you OK?

I could have told him she was not.

He went and tried to put his arm around her but she knocked him away. She started screaming things about how she had lost more babies than God and no one made a religion out of *her*. I asked her if she wanted me to go get Daddy and she said That's right you go get that Daddy of yours, he'll do whatever you say. You have everything a man wants don't you, those perky little bosoms of yours and all that new blood just waiting to make babies, you're all set to take over.

I started saying No ma'am I'm not and she said Don't no ma'am me! She grabbed me by the hair with both her hands and started yanking. Showing off, coming in here all curlyhaired, I'll show you what it's like to be Bill Campbell's wife!

She grabbed the scissors and cut off all the hair she was yanking with her other hand. My brother was crying and yelling Stop it, stop it! Then she turned on him and said I'll give you something to cry about! She came at him with the scissors but before she got to him I kicked her hard in the leg. When she lost her balance we got away. We slammed the door behind us and she stayed put. There wasn't a sound coming from in there.

Now I have a big place on the side of my head with no hair. It's ugly and there is no way to hide it. I don't look like myself in the mirror. My eyes are flat. All they are doing is looking out. What they see stays right where it is. Nothing can come in.

This morning I went to talk to the box children in the closet and they were gone, box and all. I looked every place there was to look. In the towels, under all the beds, in the drawers, on top of tall things, everywhere. Finally I sat down at the kitchen table and tried to think of what Mother might have done with them. I guess maybe she knew who they were all along.

Then I thought I heard Help! Help! and when I followed the noise it took me to the kitchen garbage can. There they were in the bottom, all covered over with thrown-away food. I would've burned them up when I did the trash if they hadn't screamed for their lives, and if I hadn't heard them.

When I was taking them back to the closet I looked out the window and saw Mother climbing into the old refrigerator out back. I saw her pull the door closed. I'm sure she knew it wouldn't open from the inside, since only the new ones have that feature. I ran right out after her. I saw a trail of blood dripped on the sidewalk in a line right up to the refrigerator door.

I opened it up and there was Mother in there. All the shelves were out and she was sitting in the bottom holding on to a bloody bundle. Blood was all over. She had on the maternity blouse and a bloody skirt and her face was white.

She said Close the door Lou Ann. This is none of your business.

I started grabbing her out but she fought me hard. Finally when she bit me I let her go. CLOSE THE GOD-DAM DOOR! she said.

Is that the baby? I said.

It's a dead one, she said. Lucky you, another baby for your goddam box. Shut the door and leave me alone.

I shut the door.

After a minute she said, Lou Ann honey, are you still out there? I didn't answer. I don't know why.

Open the door sweetheart, I need to tell you something, then you can close it right back if you want to, she said.

I waited.

Lou Ann? Lou Ann? Are you there?

Open this door right this minute! Do you hear me? Open it!

Please honey? I need you to do this for me. Please?

Then just crying sounds.

I waited even longer. It took a while for me to think that she could really die in there. Then it took a while to see how I felt about that. Part of me wanted it so much. Just the simpleness of it. Her, gone.

Then she started using her low crackly voice. When I get out of here I will make you wish you had never been born, she said.

I think if I was going to wish that I would have already.

You will go straight to hell for this, she said.

So will you, I said.

Hell doesn't scare me, she said.

I thought of her in hell. She would be running the place in no time. Then she said, The thing is I can't seem to stop bleeding. I'm making a real mess in here. If you clean it up now it won't be too bad, but later things will start to smell. Think about it.

She started coughing.

Finally I opened the door and pulled her out. She was hanging on to the bundle with one arm and trying to smooth down her bloody dress with the other. She stood up as straight as she could and walked real slow over to the trash barrel. Don't tell your father, she said. Then she put the bundle in with the burned trash. She said Go get some rags so you can get started on all this.

My voice came out so deep I wasn't sure it was me. You made the mess, I said. You clean it up.

I went straight to get the bundle out of the trash. Mother tried to stop me but instead she fainted to the ground. I couldn't make her wake up.

There was nobody around to help.

I could see Les out in the far corner of the field in front of the house so I got in the car and started driving through the dirt. I put the bundle on the seat beside me.

Les stopped the tractor and ran over when I got close and he saw it was me. I told him Mother had the baby dead. He got in and drove us as fast as he could. He pulled the car up in back. Mother was right there in the dirt where I left her. I had halfway thought she might be inside making lunch with the mess all cleaned up. Then when I walked in with Les she'd say, Don't believe a word Lou Ann tells you, she's always making trouble.

Les laid her down in the back seat of the car. It's a good thing we have plastic seat covers. He asked if I wanted to come but I said no. He said to give him the bloody bundle but I said Please let me keep it, and he did.

After he left I opened it up.

At first I could only see a bloody jelly mess. But I knew the baby was in there so I wasn't afraid to look harder. I had to feel into it with my fingers to find him.

He looked like the tiny see-through bird bodies inside sparrow eggs that the wind blows down onto the sidewalk before it's time for them to hatch.

I wrapped him back up and left him on the steps while I got the box children. Until then they had never met an actual dead baby. It was an honor for all of us.

We named him Richard. We buried him out by the rose bush. It was a long time before we stopped crying.

Daddy got home in the late afternoon with a new air compressor in the back of the pickup. He was up to the porch before he saw the blood dripped out to the refrigerator, and the big sticky place where Mother had been bleeding on the ground. By then it was more of a brown than a red.

When I told him Les had taken Mother, he ran right back out to his pickup and drove off. He didn't even take the air compressor out. I hope it doesn't get stolen. I sat on the steps with the box children until dark when Buck and Lonnie and my brother came in for supper. There wasn't any because I forgot to make it.

I told them what happened except for the part of me leaving the refrigerator door closed a long time. Buck got the big flashlight and went out to clean up the blood. That is the last of Richard I will ever see.

Lonnie sat with me on the steps and put his arm

around my shoulder. My brother went into the house and didn't come back out.

After a while Les pulled up in our car. He brought a big bag of cheeseburgers from the Sunrise Cafe, and sweet rolls for in the morning. He said Loretta is OK but the baby never had a chance and there won't be any more after this. Nature isn't perfect, he said. Mother has to stay a few days and Daddy is staying with her.

I sat out with the hired hands and ate cold cheeseburgers in the dark. We saw the Big Dipper and the Great Bear. Then I went to bed. That is were I am writing from. It's just me and my brother in the house, and the box children. I do not remember ever feeling this much sadness or this much calm.

Tuesday, August 16, 1960

Last night I heard my brother crying on the back porch bed. Just little sobs. They kept on for a while.

I put a shirt on over my nightgown and went out there. I said What's the matter?

He just kept sobbing. I sat down on the side of the bed. Finally he said he had a bad dream. He was going out in the night to shut off the windmill saying I'm not afraid

I'm not afraid I'm not afraid, and when he went to pull down the bar a big hairy man jumped out and grabbed him and yelled OH YES YOU ARE! The man wouldn't let go. My brother woke up crying.

He asked me to turn on the light so I did. After a while the crying stopped. He asked if I think Mother and Daddy are really coming back.

I said Sure, don't you? He said maybe we had been too much trouble for them. I said I thought they were too much trouble for us.

My brother said, I thought Daddy was the boss of things but it turned out he isn't.

Sometimes he is, I said. He just has to keep on the right track with Mother.

My brother said, Bosses don't have to keep on the right track. They own the track.

It was quiet for a while. Then I said, I never did mean for you to get in trouble over that song.

He acted like he didn't hear me and I thought maybe he was still mad. But then he said I didn't mean you any harm either Lou Ann. He started crying again. He said Everything's so different from how it was. All I ever do now is drive around in circles on a hot tractor. It seems like things happen all around wherever you go and nothing ever happens to me.

Maybe you're lucky, I said. Half the things that happen to me I wish did not. I tried to laugh to make him feel better.

Then he said Did you really want that new baby?

More than anything, I said.

Not me, he said. I think there's enough of us.

After a while he said Would you stay out here with me, in case the dream comes back?

I said maybe we could make a pallet on the living room floor like when we were little, pretending we were camping out. So we took all the covers off both our beds and made one comfy pile for him and one for me. I left the hall light on.

Right before I fell asleep I said I'm glad you're my brother. He said Goodnight sis. We neither one woke up til this morning when Les came in with the sweet rolls.

Now the men, and my brother who I now know is not really a man yet just because he has to work like one, are back in the field and I am sitting at the kitchen table. I got Lonnie to bring me back my diary and I'm looking at it here in a pile. There is a lot. I don't want to read it yet. I think for now I will just keep on going.

With no one in the house but me it's easy to think. Mother could have run out of air and she would have cried out but no one would have heard a thing. Daddy would have come home and found his wife and baby dead in the old refrigerator he put there. Daddy Wayne would have kicked him off the farm and taken my brother and me away. I kept all that from happening.

Sometimes when Mother used to get mad she would say, You wouldn't even be alive if it weren't for me. Now I can say the same to her. It changes everything.

I don't know what will happen next. When Mother and Daddy come home I am sure they will try to get things back to normal. But I am not on either side of their war. I'm on my own side now.

I got a postcard from Earl today. I was not expecting that. It has a picture of downtown Kansas City. It says: Hey Lou Ann! Thinking of you all in K.C. We got rained out where we were cutting so we came on into the city for some fun. Nobody's wheat around here looks as good as your Daddy's. Save me a peach! Your friend, Earl.

Now I have gotten mail from Oklahoma City and Kansas City. Does every state have a city named after it? If so I would like to have a letter from all of them. Maybe someday I will take a grand tour. Maybe Earl and me can start our own company of cutters and I can be like Mrs. Cumberland, traveling around and cooking for all the Wheaties in the trailers.

I know that's way off in the future but it's not impossible. And if it was impossible I wouldn't need to know that right now. It's better just to keep going ahead with things you think might happen. That alone can get you pretty far, and by the time you get to the impossible place you might decide you wanted something else anyway.

On the other hand, sometimes it's important to give up. Like when Alva says she doesn't have a mama. It makes it easier. She knows it's her own job to get the things she needs.

I am using her for a model. I have made a hard place in my heart about my mother and Daddy. I don't know if I will ever let the softness grow back.

In the meantime there are some things I need:

1. My own lock box. I will be the only one with a key.
2. Lots of spiral writing notebooks.
3. My own stamps for letters.
4. A dollhouse for the box children to live in, and a new doll to live with them, six in all. It needs to be a nice big house with lots of furniture and toys and a watchdog for protection, one that bites.
5. Storebought dresses. I will be the one to pick them out.
6. Water to waste for baths all by myself. And water

for the rose bush and the flowers I will plant on top of Richard.

7. Locks on the doors to the bathroom and my bed-room.
8. My own supply of sanitary conveniences. I could start up red again any day now.
9. Visits from friends any time they want to come.

I can keep adding to the list when I think of other things. Some of them will cost money, which I'm saving up starting with the four dollars Mother never did remember to ask for. Some will cause fights, but that is OK with me. I will win right out if I can or else I will sneak and hide and wait until the way gets clear to what I want.

The air is changing towards cooler. The fields are deep brown and ready for planting. I'm sitting out on the front porch steps with the box children, holding them up to see. They are more sure about life now than they have ever been. If they could choose again, they would.

Acknowledgments

Writing itself is solitary, but my life is not at all. There are many people whose belief and support helped me write this book.

The writing helpers: Lisa Shea is my writing mentor and I will forever be grateful for her skill, heart, and friendship. The attention of Carole Houck Smith made me believe I could write a novel, and her reading helped shape the outcome. Thomas Talbot gave great writing assignments, and pieces I wrote for his class morphed into parts of this book. The International Women's Writing Guild, founded and led by Hannelore Hahn, gave me a place to start and enabled me to connect with my agent. Two teachers, Ellen Knighton and Martha Acker, inspired and encouraged me long ago.

The writing friends: Therese Stanton and Anastasia Higginbotham. Their names are complete sentences.

The Sunday afternoon writers—Dorothy Fain, Linda Ostreicher, Larry Woodbridge and Phebe Brown, and also

Ann Starer, Amy Waterman, and Paula Curran—helped keep me going for more than ten years.

The writing books: Natalie Goldberg's *Writing Down the Bones*, Brenda Euland's *If You Want to Write*, and Dorothea Brande's *Becoming a Writer* were vital to me.

My agent, Meredith Bernstein, sold this book with a passion. Wendy Carlton, my editor at Riverhead, is very smart and good at what she does. I feel lucky to be working with her.

The best, most concentrated, and productive writing times of my life have been at Ragdale, and I am very grateful to The Ragdale Foundation for two summer fellowships. I also did important writing for this book at My Retreat, Cora Schwartz's haven. I finished it in the apartment of Glen Sanford and Jessie Beckett.

Glen is my son, and his faith in me has made all the difference.

I thank my not-for-profit clients in New York City—Educational Equity Concepts, Girls Incorporated, and Metro International—for doing important work and paying me to help. I thank the old Saturday night group at Grace Church, and Lois W. I thank the writers Ellen Bass and Laura Davis, E. Sue Blume, Judith Hermann, Polly Berrien Berends, and Alice Miller. I thank the Birthday Bash women—Andrea Nemetz, Stacey Simon, Margaret Shiba, Marcela Hahn, Amy Plotch, Ann Starer, Ellen Taus, Sharon Blume, Joan Beard, Elinore Antell, Diane Roberts, Amy Waterman, and Marjorie

Morrow—for years of friendship and celebration of all our successes. I thank Susan Mufson for her counsel and knowledge. I thank the amazing Mike Warren for helping me find my singing voice. I thank Denise DeYonker for bringing order out of chaos. I thank Tom and the rest of the team at Connecticut Muffin in Park Slope. I thank Prospect Park and the old waffle iron at Camille's on Henry Street. I thank Steve Sanford, Stanley Bosworth, Barbara O'Rourke, Josh Michtom and Mike Esper. I thank Dorchen Leidholdt, Andrea Dworkin, Merle Froschl, and Barbara Sprung. I thank Marsha Newton, Catherine Brumley, Jan Loe, Kathleen Atteberry, Diane Barclay, and Rebecca Rolon.

I thank my mother, father, sister, and brother for their love and support over all the years.

I thank time, life, trees, bees, and the moon.

I thank my husband, David Satz, for his love, support, encouragement, understanding, humor, leaf-catching, and funny dancing; I thank him for being the right one, and for coming along.

And I thank you, reader. I've needed you to be there.